MW01284005

THOMAS JEFFERSON

Lessons from a Secret Buddha

SUNEEL DHAND

MINDSTIR MEDIA

Published by Mindstir Media
PO Box 1681 | Hampton, New Hampshire 03843 | USA
1.800.767.0531 | www.mindstirmedia.com

Printed in the United States of America

ISBN-13: 978-0-9836771-2-3

Library of Congress Control Number: 2012935454

Visit Suneel Dhand on the World Wide Web:
www.suneeldhand.com

To my parents, without whom no achievement in my life would be possible, and to whom I owe everything that is best in me

I had become a physician to help cure illness and disease, but after a few years in practice, I began to realize that a significant number of the health problems that we face in society are the result of poor lifestyle choices. My interest in well-being began with that simple realization. No doubt, modern medicine is amazing and we can now cure previously incurable diseases with miraculous new treatments, but at the same time, there just seemed to be so much preventable illness out there.

The terms "wellness" and "well-being" are interesting. The World Health Organization describes them in both physical and emotional terms. They certainly involve a combination of factors, but what are they exactly?

I started researching all the components that could truly help one attain well-being, reading everything I could find and meeting with many experts across the country. The advice ranged from simple diet and exercise to mindset and attitude. My work was published and I became quite well known. Then one day I received an e-mail from my old Harvard professor and spiritual mentor.

My Old Friend,

I hope this e-mail finds you well. I have been reading your articles and am very impressed with your findings. But rather than looking at all the evidence, why not get your example directly from a master himself? I have a secret to share with you. Can you meet me at the Starbucks on School Street next Tuesday at 8 pm?

Yours,

Prof

Ten days later I found myself on a plane to Nepal to meet a mysterious, secluded group of sages whose community had lived in near isolation for hundreds of years. In that Boston coffee shop, my professor had introduced me to the astonishing new discoveries that had been made about these people. Nestled in the Himalayas, protected from invasions over the centuries, they had formed a remarkable civilization, well ahead of their time. They had secretly traveled far and wide and taught numerous people. I saw a preview of their ancient practices, scientific texts, and research—and was excited about meeting them. Unfortunately, their numbers had now dwindled to just a dozen or so.

I was taken on a bumpy seven-hour drive from the airport up toward the majestic towering mountains that define that part of the world. I arrived at a large wooden complex, halfway up one of the mountains, and was led inside. The first person I met was an elderly man, who greeted me with a warm and friendly handshake. He sat down opposite me while another sage, dressed in the same simple red-orange clothing, poured some tea. I got right to the point and told him what I had heard about their people, how my professor had emphasized their unique lifestyle, and how I wanted to discuss ways in which they could probably help many others with their teachings.

The gentleman handed me a large, ancient-looking book, along with a box containing a number of handwritten letters. I glanced through them; some appeared to be long letters, while others were shorter notes. They all looked so old, I worried that the paper might crumble in my hands. The words that came next I never could have dreamed of.

"Look no further than your own countryman, the great Mr. Thomas Jefferson," he said with shining eyes.

"The president?" I replied.

"Yes, the president. How much do you really know of him?"

I knew he was one of the earliest presidents, having lived sometime around the Revolution. Immortalized in history and a true American legend.

"Yes, he was a very gifted man. . . . But there is a secret."

I listened attentively.

"He was a meticulous writer who documented everything he did in all of his letters and correspondences. But *one* set of letters was confiscated soon after the Revolution. These letters have now come back into our possession from the archives, thanks to a trusted and well-connected friend."

"Have you ever read anything about Thomas Jefferson's mother, Mrs. Jane Jefferson?" the other, much younger sage seated next to him asked me.

I hadn't.

"You won't find much. The name of Jane Jefferson has all but been removed from history. Does this not strike you as odd, considering that she came from a well-to-do family and had such a famous son?"

I nodded, encouraging them to go on.

"You see, both Thomas Jefferson and his mother were followers of one of our people. A very wise and noble man—one of our greatest leaders. We called him Buddha Bhai."

"As in the religion?" I asked.

"Not in that sense. There is no suggestion that either Tom or his mother were anything other than Christians, as the history books tell us. You see, back in those days, anything considered remotely foreign and different was frowned upon and to some extent feared."

"Who was this person?" I asked.

"I will get to that. *Buddha* simply means an Enlightened One. *Bhai* means brother. Our people have always been explorers. In the late eighteenth century, we were escaping a tyrannical neighboring king who would stop at nothing to destroy our people. Many wandered westward and were able to travel all the way to the Americas by boat. Inevitably, they also encountered many wonderful people along the way."

I sat transfixed.

The sage placed his cup of tea on the table in front of me. "Let me tell you a story. . . ."

I

The colonies of America had been in existence for over 150 years, since the first settlement established at Jamestown. A steady flow of hope-filled people had made the brave journey across the Atlantic, ready to start life afresh in the New World. Encompassing a large swath of the Eastern seaboard, they were now rapidly expanding westward toward the Appalachian Mountains.

- Virginia, established 1607
- Massachusetts, 1620
- New Hampshire, 1623
- Maryland, 1634
- Connecticut, 1635
- Rhode Island, 1636
- Delaware, 1638
- North Carolina, 1653
- South Carolina, 1663
- New York, 1664
- New Jersey, 1664

- Pennsylvania, 1682
- Georgia, 1732

All thirteen colonies appeared to be amicably coexisting with their mother country across the Atlantic. They were heading for victory in the frontier wars, pushing back against the French, with Spain's influence in North America dwindling. But beneath the surface, tension was simmering.

It was a stormy time for a fifteen-year-old boy named Thomas Jefferson to be growing up.

Tom was born in Shadwell, Albemarle County, Virginia, on April 13, 1743 (April 2 by the old Julian calendar, which switched to the Gregorian calendar in 1752). His mother, Jane, was born into modest means in England, her family actually having descended from English and Scottish aristocracy. His father, Peter Jefferson, was a self-made land surveyor and planter. Tom, the third of ten children, had a comfortable and happy childhood. From an early age, however, it was clear that Tom was no ordinary boy. Although shy and sensitive, his eagerness to learn astounded everyone. When all of his brothers and sisters were playing together outside, Tom was at his parents' side asking them questions about the world around him. He always preferred the company of adults, who seemed so much more interesting and fun to him than his peers.

At just six years of age, Tom was already absorbing his father's book collection and learning the violin. Only three years later, he had exhausted most of the house library and was studying Greek, Latin, and French. He had mastered these languages by the time he was fourteen, when tragedy struck. Peter Jefferson passed away suddenly. Tom had always been especially close to his father. One of his favorite pastimes growing up had been going with his father on trips into the country and meeting Indians. He was devastated by the loss and sank into a deep depression.

Only a year later, Tom was a mere shadow of the bright young boy he had once been. He was in school in Gordonsville and his teacher, Reverend James Maury, was disappointed with the abrupt decline. His mother, who was also taking care of his siblings, worried incessantly that he was not turning into the young man she and Peter had expected. Tom had stopped studying, routinely missed many of his classes, and had put on a large amount of weight—to the point that he was barely recognizable. He complained constantly of feeling tired, regularly reporting ailments such as coughs and colds. Tom spent much of his time locked up in his room, but when he did venture out, he was mixing with the wrong company and frequently getting himself into trouble.

"When I recollect that at fourteen years of age the whole care and direction of myself was thrown on myself entirely, without a relation or friend qualified to advise or guide me, and recollect the various sorts of bad company with which I associated from time to time, I am astonished I did not turn off with some of them and become as worthless to society as they were."

One cloudy spring Saturday afternoon in the Virginia countryside, Tom was enjoying a day of leisure with his friends. The boys had been playing cards, gambling, amusing themselves with pranks, and riding their horses in the woods. They tired by early evening, and Tom had promised his mother he would be home by sunset. He had given himself ample time to make the hour-long journey.

Bidding good-bye to his three friends, Tom headed southward toward his home in Shadwell. The clouds had grown more menacing as the day wore on, and he was no more than a quarter mile down the well-beaten path when the rain started, light at first but soon pelting down more vigorously. The dirt road was difficult to navigate at the best of times, but the rain soon turned the dirt to mud, making it even harder to travel. A streak of blinding lightning followed by deafening thunder was enough to startle his horse into bolting. Tom was hurled into the air. He landed on the ground with a thud, his body twisted. Terrible pain seared his right leg, and blood trickled across his forehead.

He lay groaning in agony for not more than a few minutes when he heard another horse approaching, its hoofs squelching in the mud. It came to a halt next to him. Tom felt a presence lean over his twisted, muddied body and gently turn him over. He opened his eyes and a blurry figure came into view. A warm hand gently wiped his forehead and poured a sweet-smelling lotion onto it. Tom's eyes opened more fully and he could now see the mysterious stranger more clearly. The man, who was dressed in peculiar orange-red attire, tended to Tom's injuries and then offered to take him back home on his horse.

Tom had never seen anyone like him before. He didn't appear to be a European or a Native Indian or an African.

Tom immediately began to feel better; fortunately his injuries were not terribly serious. The rain soon eased and the path home grew less treacherous. The two talked the whole way back, Tom recounting his upbringing and recent troubles, the stranger asking many questions but saying little of himself. Tom was struck by the man's warmth and kindness, and felt unusually comfortable talking to him. He asked for his name as he was dropped off at his gate.

"You can call me Bhai," he said in his unusual accent as he rode away before anyone else could catch a glimpse of him.

A week later Tom's mother handed him a letter over the breakfast table.

May 18, 1758

Dear Thomas,

It was a pleasure to have helped you that day. I could tell that you are a remarkable young man, but I worry for your well-being. You told me that your life has gone somewhat awry since the passing of your father, for which I am very sorry. It is obvious from what you said that you are not taking the right care of yourself and have been mixing with the wrong people. You also asked when we met if I could share more about my culture with you. I found you unusually intelligent and curious for your age. I am happy to share my culture with you, for I believe what I have to tell may be able to help you too. When the student is ready the teacher appears. You can search throughout the entire universe for someone who is more deserving of your love and affection than you are yourself, and that person is not to be found anywhere. You yourself, as much as anybody in the entire universe, deserve your love and affection.

Yours,

Buddha Bhai

A few days later, another letter was handed to Tom.

May 22, 1758

Dear Thomas,

My people are from the East, thousands of miles across the ocean, near the splendor of the Himalayas. We have lived there for many centuries, and our civilization has thankfully been spared from many of the surrounding invasions. Unfortunately, we have fallen on difficult times of late, and have been threatened by tyranny of the worst form. Few know of our existence. Many of us *now travel the world, seeking to advance ourselves and help make positive change. The reason we are here in the Americas I cannot yet tell you, for your own safety too. I hope you will forgive me for being so secretive.*

Our people practice a unique way of living, founded on age-old principles. Originally Buddhists, a religion thousands of years old, our main practices are still very much similar, but we have formed our own beliefs over time. In fact, we are now scholars of all world religions, since we believe them to be the same at their core, all seeking to advance the cause of humanity. All doors leading to the same beautiful room. Creating divisions is something we seek not to partake in. In the sky, there is no distinction of east and west; people create distinctions out of their own minds and then believe them to be true. I shall write again soon and share with you our timeless Ancient Principles.

Yours,

Buddha Bhai

Tom was delighted to receive the letters and still fascinated by the mystical and intriguing gentleman. He had grown increasingly frustrated with the turn his life had taken over the last year—perhaps this kind stranger really could help him? He kept the letters secret, sharing them only with his best friend, Dabney Carr, as the two rode their horses together to the mountains overlooking Charlottesville. (Carr was one of his few friends who was not a bad influence.) Three weeks later a third letter arrived.

June 12, 1758

Dear Thomas,

The First Ancient Principle is to worship your body and take great care of it always. Your body is your temple. Everything that is asked of you, from physical activity to thought, requires a healthy body. I caught a glimpse of your prized horse, which was indeed a very fine specimen. No doubt that horse was meticulously raised. Think then, if we are inclined to take such dedicated care of our horses, should we not also do so for ourselves?

I have no doubt that a major reason why you have become apathetic and put on weight is that you are not taking the right care of your temple. Resolve to nourish yourself better. Our people believe that the best foods come directly from the soil of this beautiful Earth. I talk about the abundance of vegetables and fruits that we are blessed with. Centuries of experience have taught us that such foods are the best for our health. We are vegetarians, and do not eat meat. I understand that this concept is not familiar to your people as yet, so you may be a little surprised at this thought. But if you endeavor to eat more fruits and vegetables, you shall not be disappointed with the diversity of tasty and versatile foods available. We put much effort into how we prepare our meals, and seek to enjoy them as much as possible. Furthermore, we are sure to eat only in moderation, and avoid the bad habit of overindulgence.

Please also pay careful consideration as to what you put into your temple in other ways—seek to avoid any further such *intakes which may be harmful. To keep the body in good health is a duty . . . otherwise we shall not be able to keep our mind strong and clear.*

Yours,

Buddha Bhai

Tom usually had a wide array of extravagant dishes prepared by his family cooks. Like most youngsters, he had always eaten whatever was put in front of him, with little attention paid to what was on his plate. He had never had any particular affinity to vegetables or fruits, any more so than all the other foods he had grown up eating. Nevertheless, Bhai's ideas sounded so unusual that he was interested in trying them for himself.

The very next morning, he rode his horse down to the bustling food market in the center of Shadwell and purchased a basketful of fresh vegetables: carrots, artichokes, broccoli, asparagus, and kale. Tom handed these to his cooks, who looked perplexed when he asked them to prepare his dinner using only those vegetables. That evening, he was given a bland stew, not very appealing to his eye or satisfying to his taste buds. The same thing happened the following day. Tom replied to the address at the top of Bhai's letter, to vent his skepticism.

June 28, 1758

Dear Thomas,

You need to be more creative with the preparation, since this is not a habit your people are used to. I expect to be in your area again by the end of summer and shall be in touch. In the meantime, keep trying, and when I arrive I want to be able to try some of your creations!

Yours,

Buddha Bhai

For the next few weeks, Tom continued making his requests of the cooks—bringing home even more fresh produce from the same market on his way home from school. The rich, fertile soil of Virginia allowed for the abundant growth of vegetables and fruits, so they were easily available from the local merchants. Tom asked for them to be cooked in as many different ways as possible: steamed, boiled, roasted, garnished, sautéed—alone or as part of other dishes. He found the task challenging but was committed to making them more appealing, unlike the bland vegetables he had grown up with.

To the astonishment of his mother, he even started experimenting with cooking himself, using different herbs and seasonings. Tom tried every vegetable and fruit he could get hold of: eggplant, cauliflower, lettuce, spinach, onions, potatoes, corn, kidney beans, okra, squash, figs, apples, peaches, cherries, pears, plums, apricots, berries, and tomatoes. (There was a widespread rumor at the time that tomatoes were poisonous, and on one occasion Tom caused quite a stir when he ate one in front of his family.) Two of his favorites became peas and cucumbers. He mixed and matched, cut and mashed, added the herbs and seasonings, made pies, soups, omelets, salads, desserts, and a new macaroni vegetable casserole. Very soon, the exotic dishes were the talk of the whole household, and Tom was proud to show off his novel way of eating.

"I have lived temperately, eating little animal food, and that . . . as a condiment for the vegetables, which constitute my principal diet."

Many of the meals prepared by the cooks would be served on large, fancy platters, particularly when guests were visiting the residence. Tom, aware of his weight problem, started practicing greater temperance, eating only two main meals a day, with small snacks of fruit and tea in between.

"We seldom repent of having eaten too little."

September 1, 1758

Dear Thomas,

It was wonderful to have seen you again that afternoon and, yes, I did think your dishes were most enjoyable. Of course, in the East we use many more spices, but I do not think these will be easy for you to obtain.

Let me tell you that eating a wholesome diet is only the first part of keeping your temple in order. The second is to make sure that your body is exerted well and never left to lay idle. Our people are sure to exercise daily, usually in the mornings, helping to invigorate us for the rest of the day. We use a number of techniques, until our bodies tire and we find ourselves breathless. Please see attached to this letter my sketches detailing our daily exercises. Oftentimes we run around our village, uphill, for sometimes an hour every day in groups.

You mentioned that you had a farming upbringing, and an agricultural life is certainly amongst the best for exercise. My grandfather himself was a farmer, the most sturdy of men, spending hours every day toiling in the fields. Leading a life of physical slumber will make you lazy and lead you to putting on weight and growing bigger, amongst the worst of all human afflictions. We are blessed with the ability to move swiftly. Even when you walk, walk briskly, and upright.

So endeavor to give yourself plenty of physical exercise at every opportunity. Youthfulness may temporarily negate many bad *habits, but as one gets older, the First Ancient Principle becomes more pertinent.*

Yours,

Buddha Bhai

Tom's new dietary habits had already visibly improved his weight, although he was still not as trim as he used to be. He had never been involved in any regular exercise (in the late eighteenth century there were few organized sporting activities to participate in). Simple games and horse riding were the extent of his physical activity. Tom started in a most straightforward way, with brisk walking. Surrounded by the beautiful, lush countryside, he found no shortage of open space. The hills would test his strength. In the pleasant fall weather, Tom would walk soon after waking up, and then again in the afternoon. He was surprised at how challenging he found the sloped landscape, being left gasping for breath and exhausted after only a few minutes. But he persisted, and his stamina increased day by day.

Just before the winter snow arrived, he was able to walk briskly for at least a half hour at a time, circling the lands around his house and the center of town. Tom drew out a course for himself, often counting the number of steps and how long it would take to walk a mile. He did certainly find that he always returned from those walks feeling greatly refreshed.

During his excursions around Albemarle, Tom encountered several other townsfolk who enjoyed walking too. There was little doubt that they also appeared to be in excellent health, and none of them were overweight. Tom encouraged his family and friends to join him, yet despite his best efforts, he remained in the minority, as most people would rather use their horses than their own two legs. From that time on, Tom rode his horse only when it was absolutely necessary.

"Dispositions of the mind, like limbs of the body, acquire strength by exercise. . . . If the body be feeble, the mind will not be strong. . . . The sovereign invigorator of the body is exercise, and of all the exercises walking is best. A horse gives but a kind of half exercise, and a carriage is no better than a cradle. . . . Habituate yourself to walk very far. The Europeans value themselves on having subdued the horse to the uses of man. But I doubt whether we have not lost more than we have gained, by the use of this animal. . . . An Indian goes on foot nearly as far in a day, for a long journey, as an enfeebled white does on his horse, and he will tire the best horses. There is no habit you will value so much as that of walking far without fatigue. . . . Not less than two hours a day should be devoted to exercise."

Smoking was also becoming popular, and tobacco was grown on the family estate. The notion of filling his body with smoke repulsed Tom. He developed a strong distaste for it, refusing to participate in spite of taunts from many of his friends. He walked away whenever anyone smoked in his presence.

"Raising tobacco . . . it is a culture productive of infinite wretchedness."

As that eventful year drew to a close, Tom found that he had lost all of his excess weight as a result of his unique new lifestyle. Though he still mourned his father deeply, he was convinced that taking care of his body was helping him feel a great deal better.

II

When he was sixteen, Tom entered the College of William and Mary in Williamsburg, over one hundred miles away from Albemarle. He had some trouble adjusting to life away from home, deprived of the comforts of his upbringing. It was more difficult to get his favorite foods; vegetables and fruits around Williamsburg were not as fresh, and the college-prepared meals were woefully lacking in nutrition. Neither were the open spaces around the campus so pleasant for walking.

But once those first few difficult weeks were behind him, Tom befriended some of the other students, who had been sent from all over the colony. Slowly but surely, he began to enjoy his newfound freedom, and was introduced to the thriving college social scene. There were countless opportunities to attend regular parties and organized events, such as horse racing and kite-flying competitions. He joined a number of exclusive clubs, most devoted strictly to leisure activities. His new socialite friends were very different from the ones he had in Albemarle. They came from the elite families of Virginia and had a penchant for high living (but no great love for working). The pleasures and temptations of this student life overwhelmed Tom, taking precious time away from his studies.

One semester came to an end—then two—then three. Before he knew it, the first year had flown by, without any significant academic accomplishment. His grades were merely average.

June 19, 1760

Dear Thomas,

I am glad to hear that you are still enjoying eating more earthly foods and also experiencing significant benefits from your daily walks. I am not surprised that you feel so much the better for it. I was, however, most disappointed when you told me of your recent love for pleasures and distaste for books, especially since it was a pastime that you enjoyed so much when you were a boy. I hope that this is just a temporary phase for you, because you do indeed have so much potential. Just as a flower will wither if it does not get watered, so your mind will diminish and not prosper if you do not feed it with constant knowledge.

The Second Ancient Principle is just this very belief. To always keep a great thirst for knowledge. The ability to learn is our greatest talent. It is indeed the only separation between us and animals. I return to the analogy of your horse. A horse today is exactly the same as a horse from a thousand years ago. It shall eat, run, and sleep. And that horse even the same as a thousand years before that. But look at us, Thomas, we lead very different lives from those who came before. Our ancient ancestors took the decision to leave the cave. They built villages and towns. Then they crossed land and took to the seas. Do you doubt that one day we will also take to the skies? Each generation must be better than the one that precedes it. The only reason we shall progress is that we are learned creatures, who are able to advance ourselves and our surroundings. Your mind is a wonderful gift from God, and to leave it empty and not working is a terrible waste. You can certainly enjoy pleasures, but never at the expense of your studies.

My people encourage diligent reading of all types of works. We devote as many hours as possible to this pursuit from the earliest age, because education and knowledge is the paramount cornerstone of any society. There is no answer that cannot be found in a book. Whatever you are looking for, somebody has already experienced and written about it. The book is your best friend.

Yours,

Buddha Bhai

As Tom reflected upon that wasted year of college and his mediocre grades, he felt somewhat guilty—more so when his disappointed mother saw his report letter and reminded him how much the family was spending on his education. He was certainly capable of doing much better, and he knew it.

July 10, 1760

Dear Thomas,

It was a terrific afternoon walking with you on your beautiful estate. You can keep those books for as long as you desire. Keep in mind, too, that the quest for knowledge and being a learned person is also about absorbing everything else around you. There is a lot to be gained from other people and from nature itself. Be a curious and questioning person, and never take it as a given that anything should be the way it is. The boundaries we set on our minds are all self-imposed.

Yours,

Buddha Bhai

Tom had planned to use his free summer back home enjoying the warm weather and outdoor leisure pursuits. Instead he resolved to make up for lost time. He had already read most of the books in his family's large collection at home, so he decided to broaden his knowledge base by borrowing books from family friends around Albemarle (all of his father's old contacts), walking them back home in his saddlebag.

The first book was a short story on ancient Greece. He read it in just two days. Then there was an anecdote on ancient Rome, which he finished in just one day, followed by *Paradise Lost* by John Milton and the works of Shakespeare. Tom realized that he could read multiple books simultaneously, devoting mornings, afternoons, and evenings to different genres.

He read for hours on end each day, devouring any book he could lay his hands on. His mother, when she wandered into his room, was greatly impressed at how he was choosing to spend his vacation. From the classic novels to books on philosophy, mathematics, astronomy, and horticulture—nothing was beyond his scope that summer.

But there was one subject that began to fascinate Tom above all others: *science*. It was the time of the Enlightenment, when reason and logical thought were promoted above the old beliefs of superstition and unproven theory. New discoveries were coming to the forefront, and as Tom read about them, he sensed that huge changes to everyday life were on the horizon. Isaac Newton and John Locke became two of his favorite authors. Much of the science he learned could now be applied to the world around him. He began to keenly observe nature—plants, trees, birds, and the weather—during his walks.

"Nature intended me for the tranquil pursuits of science, by rendering them my supreme delight. . . . No two men can differ on a principle of trigonometry. . . . There is not a sprig of grass that shoots uninteresting to me."

When the time approached to return to Williamsburg, Tom would be found in his room voraciously reading for up to fifteen hours a day, sitting on the floor with dozens of books laid out around him. Once again, reading was his favorite pastime.

"I cannot live without books. . . . Knowledge indeed is a desirable, a lovely possession."

He returned to college with a renewed passion for learning and threw himself into his studies. The many social activities he participated in during the first year were now only an occasional treat for him, as he vowed to make the most out of his remaining time at William and Mary. One lecturer, Professor William Small, was delighted with the turnaround, noting that rarely had he seen a student improve as much as Tom did from that second year onward.

November 23, 1760

Dear Thomas,

Those books on ancient history sound interesting, but let me tell you about two more recent highly enlightened souls who played a big part in the establishment of your last two colonies. The first was Mr. William Penn, founder of Pennsylvania, and the second, Mr. James Oglethorpe, founder of Georgia.

Mr. Penn was born in London, England. He was the son of a celebrated military commander, but from an early age displayed an avid interest in spirituality. To the dismay of his father, he became a Quaker as a young man. He preached peace and harmony, believing very strongly in religious freedom and expression. Sadly, he was imprisoned six times, including in the dreaded Tower of London, for refusing to renounce his beliefs. He later established the colony of Pennsylvania, which bears his name, founded on the simple principles of equality, virtue, and respect. All Mr. Penn wanted were democratic and fair ideals, with no persecution of minority beliefs.

Mr. James Oglethorpe is another brilliant Englishman. He started as a military general and then became a great philanthropist. He was horrified when he saw the routine imprisonment of debtors and the harsh prison conditions they were subjected to in England. He desired to bring the poor of his country to the New World to live in a fairer place, and founded Georgia on these humanitarian principles.

I encourage you to read more about these two most sincere and noble of men.

Yours,

Buddha Bhai

As Tom was excelling in college, other political events were taking shape in the colonies. The British found themselves in debt from the French and Indian frontier wars. Crown and Parliament demanded extra money and turned their attention to the colonies to help them raise it. Up in Massachusetts, there was dismay over the new policy of King George III of enforcing the Navigation acts, which imposed restrictions and duties on imported goods, and the Writs of Assistance, which gave Royal officials the right to search any local properties for smuggled goods without a warrant. A local Bostonian attorney, James Otis, made a fiery speech at the Massachusetts State House, arguing against the draconian new measures. Another young lawyer in the room, John Adams, heard the riveting speech—and wondered where all of the resentment might be leading.

III

The Writs of Assistance, as unpopular as it proved to be, was just the beginning of Britain's plans to raise more revenue from the colonies. It was not long before further policies were enacted by Prime Minister Lord Grenville's Parliament. The Sugar Act enforced a tax on foreign molasses and placed restrictions on other vital goods such as lumber and iron. It also stopped the import of French wine, which many in Tom's family would drink with their meals. The Currency Act then banned the colonies from issuing any legal paper money. Attempts at evading the new rules would be tried in a special British Vice-Admiralty court in Halifax, instead of local judicial establishments.

The very foundations of the colonial economy were shaken. Colonists were baffled over the mother country's harsh treatment of them. Many local assemblies sent formal petitions to the Crown politely asking for a rethink.

Tom, steaming ahead with his education, graduated with high honors. He had not heard from Bhai for the rest of his time at college, but every so often wrote to him using the return address from his last correspondence. Then, unexpectedly, a letter arrived one morning.

May 19, 1764

Dear Thomas,

I am thrilled to hear the news of your graduation from William and Mary with such merit. Keep up the excellent work. Remember the path of knowledge never ends. As the Greek philosopher Socrates said: Wisest is he who knows that he knows nothing.

My apologies for not writing you for so long. I have been traveling and meeting many new people. We have now reached the great Mississippi River, and I must confess my total fascination with the geography of these vast, beautiful lands. Our mission, though, is still in progress.

The Third Ancient Principle is to lead a life of self-discipline. Mastering the art of discipline will enable you to be successful in everything you do. From how you go about your daily life, to achieving any long-term aspiration, one needs to understand the importance that discipline plays. You have already shown how much you are capable of academically, but real life requires much more practical skills as well. I shall share some of ours with you.

One of the most important rules we keep is to always awake early every morning. We believe in the magical power of the mornings and never slumber into a late awakening, as there is undoubtedly something about the early rays of sunlight that helps to inspire. Upon awakening, we set aside time to think carefully about all that we would like to accomplish on that day, visualizing the morning, afternoon, and evening. Typically, we put pen to paper and write down our plans, for we believe that a plan not committed to paper is no plan at all. We seek to be as productive as we can early in the day, the best time to get work done. I have already told you about our eating, exercise, and reading habits, which help keep us full of vigor and our minds active.

Keeping disciplined is especially important when we are confronted with any big task ahead of us. Many things in life can seem overwhelming, and the start will always be the hardest, such is the rule of nature. Small daily efforts have immense power when you face a mountain to climb.

And, of course, life is not all about work either. Each day we are also sure to set aside time for relaxing, pleasurable activities, and spending quality time with our families. A healthy balance is always needed.

Yours,

Buddha Bhai

When Tom returned home after graduation, he had just turned twenty-one, and his mother and siblings organized a large welcome home gathering. According to the custom of the time, a significant inheritance from his father's estate, including a valuable amount of land and property, officially became his to manage. A life of idle luxury enjoying all the comforts of the day was now his for the taking.

June 22, 1764

Dear Thomas,

You say that you have become bored of late as you find yourself back at home after college. Let me tell you a story.

A farmer approached a local wise man and complained that during the slow winter season he would feel lethargic and get very frustrated for no apparent reason at all. He asked the wise man to help him, and was promptly told that he would have to carry a full pail of water to the next town and then walk back again without spilling a drop before the wise man would give him the answer to his problem. The farmer obliged and took a couple of days to complete his task. The wise man asked him on his return whether he had felt the same way during his two-day task.

"Why, not at all, I was concentrating too hard on not spilling any water," came the reply.

"Of course that's so. You are only frustrated and lethargic

because you have nothing else to focus your mind upon!"

So Thomas, resolve to keep yourself moving. Don't stand still in life. Time is precious, and we must have an awareness and even urgency in our use of it. Foolish people are idle, wise people are diligent.

Yours,

Buddha Bhai

Tom was not yet sure what his next step in life would be. In his final year of college, he had focused on the sciences and hatched many ideas and designs for new inventions. He decided to use his time back home to put some of them into practice. He also needed to spend more time helping his mother with the management and day-to-day running of the estate. One of the first changes he made was to start getting up at the crack of dawn, as soon as he could read the hands of the clock in front of his bed.

"Whether I retire to bed early or late, I rise with the sun."

After waking, Tom would start a fire and bathe himself—a habit that was not widely practiced at the time but helped to awaken him fully. Being interested in the weather, he went outside and recorded the temperature daily at dawn, which he found to be the coldest time of day (he repeated this again at four o'clock in the afternoon, which he thought to be the hottest). Tom then noted the wind speed and precipitation, using a weathervane and a small cup he kept outside. He kept these records in a pocket notebook, where he also began keeping details on the household.

After his morning routine, including a small breakfast and long walk, he would spend some time reading and writing letters. Tom had obtained the addresses of several prominent scientists in the colonies and overseas, and began corresponding with them. The afternoon was his designing and inventing time. Tom hoped that his ideas could revolutionize how people worked and lived. He wrote letters requesting the parts for his inventions, and boxes would arrive daily by horse carriage, the couriers paid by him when they delivered.

Beginning with his very own workspace, Tom wanted to make life easier for anyone who had to work and study in an office. He despaired that people seemed to make do with such awkward furniture and rough seating methods. A number of ideas came to mind.

- a comfortable swivel chair
- a revolving bookstand
- an easy-to-use cabinet
- a user-friendly portable table that also stored letters (a "writing box")

- a machine to hang clothes on
- a calendar clock that marked the days of the week with cannonballs

For the whole afternoon, Tom would be busily wandering around carrying a number of instruments in his pockets, including tools and rulers, mulling over drawings and working to assemble different pieces together. He showed off his many inventions to family and guests alike, exciting them with his creative new prototypes.

When he took a break, he never forgot to set aside some time for recreation. After walking outdoors, his other favorite pastimes were chess, horse riding, and music. He spent the evenings practicing the violin (which he hadn't done since he was a boy) and learned to play some of the greats like Handel and Vivaldi, entertaining his family with impromptu renditions.

"Music . . . furnishes a delightful recreation for the hours of respite from the cares of the day."

Tom was managing to fit a tremendous amount into his typical day, as he made use of every available minute. By night, he was tired enough from all of his endeavors. He was sure to sleep at least five to eight hours, reading yet again before blowing out his candle.

"I never go to bed without an hour, or half hour's previous reading of something moral, whereon to ruminate in the intervals of sleep."

Tom looked back on his first few weeks after returning home from college and realized what a waste it had been that he had gotten bored so easily. He didn't have to be in school to keep a routine going. He promised that he would never again allow himself to slip into idleness—because he was at his best when he kept occupied.

"Determine never to be idle. No person will have occasion to complain of the want of time, who never loses any. It is wonderful how much may be done, if we are always doing. . . . A mind always employed is always happy. . . . The idle are the only wretched. In a world which furnishes so many employments which are useful, and so many which are amusing, it is our own fault if we ever know what ennui is. . . . Music, drawing, books, invention and exercise, will be so many resources to you against ennui."

IV

Tom relished those several months back home, master of his own hours, but had to decide upon a formal career path on which to embark. His vast array of talents gave him plenty of options. After careful consideration, and after receiving advice from several teachers, family members, and friends, he chose to study law. He would continue to pursue his scientific interests only in his spare time. Tom bade farewell to his mother, brothers, and sisters, along with all his inventions, and left again for Williamsburg—this time determined to make a bigger name for himself. George Wythe, a leading lawyer, would be his teacher. (He would later mentor many notable people, including John Marshall and Henry Clay.)

After only two classes had been completed, Wythe could already see the potential in his new star student. He asked Tom if he would like to formally clerk in his office, and then introduced him to all the local high-ranking society people, including the governor, who resided nearby. Tom quickly became a favorite of theirs and a regular guest at their lavish dinners (they had to get used to his strange requests for so many vegetables). Everyone seated around the table was astonished at the young man's grasp of knowledge. Tom, for his part, enjoyed intellectual conversation with this influential circle, and gained invaluable knowledge about the functioning of high society.

He thought of Wythe as a second father, though his real mentor remained Bhai.

The Stamp Act was passed in March 1765. All print products, including newspapers, legal documents, and even playing cards, were to require a special stamp to show that a levy had been paid to the Crown. But this new tax was different from all the previous ones that had caused such consternation—in one major way. It was the first tax *directly* imposed on the colonies. The Act had passed without the consent of a single American representative, thus setting an alarming new precedent.

May 3, 1765

Dear Thomas,

Thank you for your last letter. I am pleased that your life is progressing well. You will no doubt make a fine lawyer. I now find myself in the bustling city of Boston, and understand the local dismay at this Stamp Act. On a brighter note, I am glad to *hear of the establishment of the new medical school in Pennsylvania. I hope this is a step towards more organized education in this most important field.*

Yours,

Buddha Bhai

Nine months into his law studies, Tom received some tragic news from home. His oldest sister, Jane, had passed away after a short illness. He had been close to her and felt the loss terribly, returning immediately to Albemarle to be with his grieving family.

"The art of life is the art of avoiding pain; and he is the best pilot, who steers clearest of the rocks and shoals with which it is beset. . . . The most fortunate of us, in our journey through life, frequently meet with calamities and misfortunes which may greatly afflict us; and, to fortify our minds against the attacks of these calamities and misfortunes should be one of the principal studies and endeavors of our lives. The only method of doing this is to assume a perfect resignation to the Divine will, to consider that whatever does happen, must happen; and that, by our uneasiness, we cannot prevent the blow before it does fall, but we may add to its force after it has fallen. These considerations, and others such as these, may enable us in some measure to surmount the difficulties thrown in our way . . . and to proceed with a pious and unshaken resignation."

September 18, 1765

Dear Thomas,

*   I am deeply saddened to hear the news of your sister. I wish you and your family all the strength in the world at this difficult time. Suffering is a most unfortunate and sad part of life.*

*   Yours,*

*   Buddha Bhai*

In the absence of antibiotics, the slightest of infections could be fatal. Tom had never been impressed by any of his encounters with physicians. The practice of medicine was still primitive, and most physicians were trained in Europe, with no established medical schools in the colonies until the new institution at the University of Pennsylvania formally opened its doors. Infectious diseases like smallpox were a dreadful scourge, ravaging whole communities. Tom was frustrated by practices that did not appear to be based on science. One common treatment of the day was blood-letting, which involved deliberately allowing patients to bleed in order to rid them of illness.

"The state of Medicine is worse than that of total ignorance. . . . I would wish the young practitioner, especially, to have deeply impressed on his mind, the real limits of his art, and that when the state of his patients gets beyond these, his office is to be a watchful, but quiet spectator of the operations of nature . . . and by all the aid they can derive from the excitement of good spirits and hope. . . .

*Here then, judicious, the moral, the humane physician should
stop. Having been so often a witness to the salutary efforts which
nature makes to reestablish the disordered functions, he should
rather trust to their action, than hazard the interruption of that,
and a greater derangement of the system, by conjectural
experiments on a machine so complicated and so unknown as the
human body, and a subject so sacred as human life. . . . One of the
most successful physicians I have ever known, has assured me, that
he used more bread pills, drops of colored water, and powders of
hickory ashes, than of all other medicines put together. It was
certainly a pious fraud."*

A physician in Boston by the name of Dr. Joseph Warren was, thankfully, starting to change things. He was putting forth innovative new evidence-based ideas, such as inoculation against smallpox. When an epidemic swept through the city, Dr. Warren saved thousands of lives by advocating for vaccination. Tom heard about this new technique and, based on his own reading on medicine, was confident enough to vaccinate the rest of his family members against this dreadful illness.

*". . .The adventurous physician goes on, and substitutes
presumption for knowledge. From the scanty field of what is known,
he launches into the boundless region of what is unknown. . . . On
the principle which he thus assumes, he forms his table of nosology,
arrays his diseases into families, and extends his curative treatment,
by analogy, to all the cases he has thus arbitrarily marshaled
together."*

October 28, 1765,

Dear Thomas,

I am glad that you are now back at School in Williamsburg. Time is the best, and sometimes only, healer.

Yours,

Buddha Bhai

Anger over the Stamp Act was widespread, and local resistance began to spring up throughout the colonies. Many merchants vowed to simply boycott all British goods by evoking non-importation agreements. Newspapers and publications also rallied against the tax. In the House of Burgesses, the colonial assembly in Virginia, a young lawyer named Patrick Henry introduced a set of resolves in opposition to the principle of taxation without representation—namely that it was fundamentally wrong to impose taxes on a group of people who had no say at all in Parliament. In Boston, a businessman-brewer and brilliant political organizer named Samuel Adams, along with a number of other locals, formed a protest group, calling themselves the Sons of Liberty. They vehemently spoke out against the Stamp Act and eventually forced all Royal stamp agents to resign from their posts. Unfortunately, the antagonism soon turned violent, and the home of the chief justice was attacked.

But worse was to come. The Quartering Act was passed a few months later, forcing local populations to house and supply food to the king's troops wherever they went. This was perceived as a further deliberate insult and provocation to the colonists. Representatives from nine of the colonies met in New York and wrote a resolution to the king asking for immediate repeal of the Stamp Act and all previous acts. They agreed that such an unfair tax passed without their consent violated basic human rights. But their protests were to no avail—the Stamp Act went into effect in November.

The colonists responded by refusing to use any of the stamped paper for their daily work. Most of the required stamps were mandatory for legal transactions, so business everywhere soon ground to a halt. By the beginning of 1766, there was widespread chaos from New Hampshire to Georgia. When news of these events reached Britain, Parliament was forced into an urgent debate over what to do next. Benjamin Franklin, the distinguished writer, scientist, inventor, and now political representative from Pennsylvania, was present in the chamber to speak for his people. He made an impassioned speech warning of a monumental crisis if the situation did not change, so strong was colonial feeling against the new unfair taxes. Franklin's argument was powerful enough that King George and Parliament finally took heed. The Stamp Act was repealed.

Meanwhile, Tom was studying furiously, needing to read about every aspect of the law. Despite finding the subject intellectually stimulating, he was no longer reading entirely for pleasure and had to graduate in good time.

June 16, 1766,

Dear Thomas,

I am concerned when you tell me that you are feeling rather stressed by your studies. Let me tell you then about our Fourth Ancient Principle. This is to always endeavor to maintain a calm mind, even in the most worrisome of situations. A spirit of calmness is needed in all of our pursuits if one is to truly succeed. There is no worse state of mind than that of being anxious and ruffled.

The next time the opportunity affords you, go down to the lake on a beautiful summer's morning and observe the tranquility of its surface. Take a small rock and throw it in. Notice what happens to that peaceful surface as the waves ripple out. Imagine then that this is exactly what shall happen to your mind when it is disturbed by stress and worry. Your tranquility and inner peace disappears. In this world of ours, there is much to concern ourselves with each and every day. My own people have suffered greatly, and had it not been for our ancient techniques, we might have succumbed to such calamities. Certainly, worries will come to all in the course of life, but master your own reactions to them. Most importantly, distinguish between those things that are within, and not within your control, and learn to let go.

Yours,

Buddha Bhai

It took over a month for news of King George's repeal to reach America. Any celebrations proved premature, because in place of the Stamp Act, a new Declaratory Act was passed, affirming that the British Parliament had total power to legislate and govern over the colonies "in all cases whatsoever." This was intended as a warning to the colonists not to attempt any future resistance.

November 2, 1766

Dear Thomas,

I shall tell you about some practices that help us stay calm. They involve a technique not yet familiar to your people. Meditation. This is the very ancient art of withdrawing yourself from the outside world, and feeling the true joy of your own innermost senses. Sit cross-legged, preferably in a natural environment, and close your eyes. Take deep breaths, in and out, in and out, in and out. Focus on nothing apart from your breathing and keep your mind empty of all thoughts. You will be experiencing your true self. Do this for as long as you are able. Some of our people are capable of sitting like this for hours every day. The calming effect is amazing. Are you able to meet me outside Williamsburg central tavern, 7 o'clock in the morning on the 10th day of November so that I can show you more?

Yours,

Buddha Bhai

The Quartering Act continued to foster resentment, especially in New York, where there were regular skirmishes between soldiers and the local population. After repeated refusal to comply, Parliament suspended the New York assembly.

December 22, 1766

Dear Thomas,

I am glad that you have been practicing the meditation techniques I showed you. Keep on perfecting. They are not easy to master and will take some time. But practice it every day and you shall reap the rewards. There is another aspect of a tranquil mind that you should endeavor to achieve. This is to live in the moment. Indeed, for too much of the time, our mind is focused on another time point, and not the present. All manner of thoughts are consuming us, directed at some other imaginary time point. But what becomes of the glory of the present moment, which we can savor at any time?

Stop to take note of the extraordinary beauty of life. Savor being with the people whom you love. Take time to look at the magnificence of a tree, the green of the grass, the gentle gushing of the beautiful stream. Do not miss a second of it. There will never be such a time as the current moment, so resolve to make the most of it. There is a time and a place to think of all your worldly concerns, but never to the point where the present is completely forgotten. As strange as this may sound, the principle of living in the present is something most people do not live nearly enough. It can be quite difficult; many of my own people are still trying to perfect this. If you can gain the habit of keeping your senses and living in the moment for most of your day, you will soar to new heights in all aspects of your life.

Do not dwell in the past, worry or dream of the future— concentrate the mind and live in the present moment, as it is better to travel well than to arrive.

Yours,
Buddha Bhai

As his workload took its toll, Tom developed a number of ways to keep himself relaxed. He began to use his daily outdoor walks as a form of relaxation mindfulness, training himself to focus only on the splendor around him, not allowing any other thought to enter his mind.

"Never think of taking a book with you. The object of walking is to relax the mind. You should therefore not permit yourself even to think while you walk. But divert your attention by the objects surrounding you."

He persuaded the college to build a small greenhouse on the campus grounds, not far from his room, where he could go and sit whenever he felt a change was needed from his small study room.

The greenhouse was filled with plants and would be soothingly warm in the morning sun. Some of Tom's classes involved partaking in mock trials and debating competitions with his peers. Passions could run high, and Tom strived to stay calm during these inevitable confrontations.

"Nothing gives one person so much advantage over another as to remain always cool and unruffled under all circumstances. . . . When angry, count ten before you speak; if very angry, a hundred. . . . Take things always by their smooth handle."

A great number of his fellow students were anxious about their future prospects and what type of practice they would end up working in. Tom had simple advice for them: to just do their best and the rest would fall into place. Worrying about the future seemed a pointless activity.

"There are, indeed, gloomy and hypochondriac minds . . . disgusted with the present, and despairing of the future; always counting that the worst will happen, because it may happen. To these I say . . . how much pain have cost us the evils that never happened. My temperament is sanguine. I steer my bark with Hope in the head, leaving Fear astern. My hopes, indeed, sometimes fail; but not oftener than the forebodings of the gloomy. . . . If I am to meet with a disappointment, the sooner I know it, the more of life I shall have to wear it off."

Tom completed his law studies with distinction and was admitted to the Virginia Bar in April 1767. Shortly thereafter, he started work as a family and land lawyer back in Albemarle. His practice thrived, as clients flocked in droves to the talented young attorney. But by then, he also had other grand plans for himself outside of work. For some time he had envisioned living in a dream mountaintop home, and was now finally in a position to start overseeing its construction on his family's land.

Monticello, meaning *little mountain* in Italian, was the name he gave to this project. Tom already knew a lot about architecture from his extensive reading, and he wanted to model Monticello on a neoclassical Italian style based on the works of Andrea Palladio, the renown Italian architect who drew inspiration from ancient Greece and Rome. When he wasn't doing his day job at the law practice, Tom worked on designing all aspects of the interior and exterior of the house, including a plan for vast gardens, where he would be able to enjoy his long walks. The interior was to be very special, with unique features that would maximize the use of light and space—including mirrors, ceiling windows, and closets.

For the outside, he set aside land where he could grow his beloved vegetables and fruits. A one-thousand-foot-long garden would be organized and divided into squares by type of plant (such as "berry squares" for currants, strawberries, and gooseberries), all surrounded by a high wooden fence for protection from animals. This vegetable garden would serve a number of functions. First, it would be a natural source of his favorite food. Second, it would act as a mini scientific laboratory where he could experiment with harvesting and cultivation techniques with the aim of producing only the best possible vegetables. Third, gardening was a great way for Tom to relax. From his many contacts, he requested seeds from far and wide, planting them as soon as a workable patch of land was available—growing anything he could, from lettuces and grapes to rice and almonds.

May 12, 1768

Dear Thomas,

I love the meticulous plans for your beautiful new home and gardens that you detailed in your last letter. A man's home is his castle, and we believe that you can tell much about a person from their residence. I hope that I shall be able to see it very soon. Your idea to harvest your own vegetables is a most admirable one. Nowhere are we more in touch with nature than when we shall grow our own food.

Yours,

Buddha Bhai

Tom could regularly be seen taking a break from his law office to go home and work in the garden. He recorded all these activities in his Garden Book. The details were extraordinary. He documented dozens of different types of pea, kidney beans, and cabbage alone. Eventually he would grow over 250 varieties of vegetables and herbs and have over one thousand fruit trees on his land. Tom preferred eating only what he grew himself, for then he knew how it was harvested and the exact quality of the food. He befriended many other agricultural people who lived in the area, and the community held regular fairs, getting together and hosting friendly competitions.

One of Tom's creations that won a number of fans was his "Monticello Salad," consisting of lettuce, cress, orach, and corn. In his interactions with other farmers, Tom observed that they appeared to be the most patriotic citizens. Laborious and self-sufficient, their relationship with the earth seemed to give them a special bond to their country.

"The earth belongs to the living. . . . The soil is the gift of God to the living. . . . No occupation is so delightful to me as the culture of earth, and no culture comparable to that of the garden. . . . The greatest service which can be rendered any country is, to add a useful plant to its culture."

After the Stamp Act debacle, Parliament surmised that the best way to raise revenue would now be through indirect taxes. The Townshend Revenue Acts, named after the chancellor, were enacted—imposing new taxes on glass, paint, paper, and tea. The British were determined to maintain tighter control this time, and overhauled the Customs System in order to better enforce the duties. They also sought to make the Royal officials independent of local legislatures, requiring them to be answerable only to the Crown.

The colonists were dismayed that Parliament seemed to have learned no lessons from the Stamp Act. Many of the boycotts that had been temporarily lifted were reinstated by angry merchants. A lawyer from Philadelphia, John Dickinson, wrote *Letters from a Farmer in Pennsylvania*, which became a widely circulated pamphlet. He asserted that Parliament had no right to impose *any* taxes—direct or indirect—for the sole purpose of raising revenue.

As the boycotts spread, more ordinary people also did whatever they could to help with the resistance movement. "Daughters of Liberty" formed, and wearing homespun cloth became popular. Many pledged outright noncooperation with all Royal officials. As a result, British trade to the northern colonies was substantially reduced within just a few months.

V

The political turmoil engulfing the colonies was the talk of every kitchen table across the land. What would happen next if the two sides could not reconcile their differences?

Between Monticello and his law practice, Tom had much to keep himself busy. Politics was a topic he had always shied away from, but the escalating situation was now affecting everybody. The more he heard about the oppressive measures of the mother country, the greater his disgust grew. For the first time, he began to voice his own opinions on the matter.

"There is not in the British empire a man who more cordially loves a union with Great Britain than I do. But by the God that made me, I will cease to exist before I yield to a connection on such terms as the British Parliament propose; and in this, I think I speak the sentiments of America."

Tom had never intended to enter the political arena. He was widely respected and admired in the local community, by law clients and farmers alike, who liked what he was saying and recognized his leadership potential. At the age of just twenty-five, he was elected to represent Albemarle County in the House of Burgesses. Tom was shocked when he heard news of his election.

January 12, 1769

Dear Thomas,

I understand your surprise that you have been elected to the House, for this may not have been the path that you intended. I have no doubt you will shine and do your best for those you represent. We have been in Massachusetts helping to show the locals how to spin their own cloth. Our people have been doing this for centuries, because being totally self-sufficient and not dependent on others is most crucial for any society. On a lighter note, some of those I taught won a recent spinning-bee competition!

Yours,

Buddha Bhai

Tom arrived for his new duties to find the House humming with activity and talk of confrontation. Nowhere, though, were tensions higher than in Massachusetts, where colonists were showing utter defiance against the Townshend Acts. Sam Adams wrote a circular letter to all colonial assemblies challenging the measures directly. Such an open letter was unacceptable to Parliament. Lord Hillsborough, Britain's secretary of state for America, issued an order for all colonial governors to immediately stop endorsing the letter. The Massachusetts Assembly officially refused—by a majority of 92 to 17. On hearing about this vote, the royal governor dissolved the general court. The only legal channel for resistance in the colony was now gone.

The British authorities, however, decided that more force was necessary to suppress the dissenters. Large numbers of warships packed with soldiers began to arrive in Boston harbor. The "Redcoats," as they were known, flooded into the city. They could be seen on every street corner and were hated by locals, who derogatorily called them "Lobsterbacks" (a reference to the fact that many would be whipped by their superiors to enforce discipline). A major standoff then occurred when the *Liberty*, a ship owned by a prominent local merchant, John Hancock, was seized by Royal officials.

Back in the House of Burgesses, a decorated military veteran and wealthy landowner named General George Washington took to the floor and presented a set of resolutions that agreed with the Circular Letter and opposed any American colonists standing trial in England. Tom sat listening to the inspirational speech and was deeply impressed with Washington's demeanor.

Tensions reached a boiling point on the night of March 5, 1770. Angry protesters outside the Boston State House confronted a group of soldiers when they caught one of them being heavy-handed and aggressive with a young man for what seemed like a minor disagreement. The two sides began to taunt each other, then became more physically threatening as tempers flared. In the commotion, the soldiers fired their muskets into the crowd. Five people were killed and several others wounded.

March 6, 1770

Dear Thomas,

I have lost one of my dear colleagues, Crispus Attucks, after the terrible events in Boston. Not many know who he really is, for he has been called African by some and Native by others. He got caught up in everything and found himself in the line of fire.

Yours,

Buddha Bhai

News of the Boston Massacre spread rapidly, filling colonists with outrage over the brutal behavior of the troops toward unarmed, defenseless citizens. A talented local silversmith and Sons of Liberty member named Paul Revere produced an engraving that depicted the massacre. The sketch was reproduced and distributed, further inflaming the tensions. Governor Hutchinson was forced to withdraw British troops from the city, and Captain Thomas Preston, the soldier in charge of the unit, along with eight of his men, was arrested and charged with murder.

While local opinion demanded the severest of punishments, two Bostonian lawyers—John Adams and Josiah Quincy—agreed to defend the soldiers, believing that whatever their own allegiances, the law must prevail over mob rule. During the trial, they argued that Captain Preston and his soldiers were provoked in a heated moment of confusion after being attacked with snow, ice, and clubs. They were successful in their defense, with only two of the soldiers being charged with manslaughter, branded, and then sent back to England.

When anger over the Townshend Acts showed no signs of abating, Parliament, under the new Prime Minister Lord North, finally decided to repeal them. They also agreed not to renew the Quartering Act. Only the duty on tea would remain—partly as a symbolic statement to assert the Crown's right to tax.

Tom was hard at work in the House eagerly hearing about all the events in Boston. His personal life took an unexpected nice turn one afternoon while he was visiting a friend in Williamsburg. He was introduced to a beautiful twenty-two-year-old widow named Martha Skelton. He found her highly intelligent and knowledgeable, and was further impressed with her passion for classical music. Tom had always been shy around women, but he was so struck by this interesting young lady that he began visiting her regularly. The pair would talk about literature and listen to music together for hours. He soon fell deeply in love for the first time in his life.

"In every scheme of happiness she is placed in the foreground of the picture, as the principal figure. Take that away, and it is no picture for me."

The two married on New Year's Day 1772 at a chapel in Williamsburg. After the ceremony, they traveled by carriage in the harsh winter weather back to Monticello. The main house was still under construction, so they had to begin their married life living in a small brick building on the property.

February 1, 1772

Dear Thomas,

I congratulate you heartily on your marriage. For how long are you at Monticello? I shall be in the area soon, and would be delighted to meet you and Martha.

Yours,

Buddha Bhai

April 12, 1772

Dear Thomas,

My journey back to Virginia is a little bit more complicated than anticipated. Nevertheless, we are making steady progress.

The Fifth Ancient Principle is one of the most straightforward, but also the most enduring. Value good character above all else and practice only the best human virtues. Be honest, sincere, kind, compassionate, and gentle. Be forgiving and show empathy. From knowing you for so long, I sense that you already have most of these attributes, but your rise in life makes keeping them all the more important. Too many people become intoxicated with power. Greatness on the outside always begins within. To walk safely through the maze of human life, one needs the light of wisdom and the guidance of virtue. Just as treasures are uncovered from the earth, so virtue appears from good deeds, and wisdom appears from a pure and peaceful mind.

Yours,

Buddha Bhai

In June 1772, a customs boat, the HMS *Gaspee*, was attacked in Narragansett Bay, Rhode Island. The locals had been protesting the enforced duties and harsh treatment by customs officials. The captain of the boat was wounded and the ship burned. The British were furious and tried in vain to arrest and try the perpetrators in England. In Massachusetts, where meetings could only be held in secret, Sam Adams helped form a special Committee of Correspondence, to aid resistance efforts. Tom was also nominated to sit on a special committee with the intent of communicating with the other colonies about ongoing developments.

August 18, 1772

Dear Thomas,

I understand your feelings about the unrest. But harboring negative emotions is one of the worst and most counterproductive things that we can ever do. Scorn, deceit, jealousy, and envy destroy us from within. Your people may be at a difficult crossroads, but I also urge you to temper any personal feelings of anger or hatred. In a controversy, the instant we feel anger, we have already ceased striving for the truth, and have begun striving for ourselves. Holding on to it is like grasping a hot coal with the intent of throwing it at someone else; you are the one who gets burned. In fact, I have seen for myself some of the British soldiers and the brutal treatment that they receive from their own superiors. Many, more so in the navy, have been impressed into their cause. Perhaps victims in a way too? I am not advocating being passive to what is going on around you, quite the contrary, it is imperative to always stand up for yourself. Just channel that feeling into positive and constructive energy.

We are shaped by our thoughts, we become what we think, and with our thoughts, we make the world. If a man speaks or acts with an evil thought, pain follows him. If a man speaks or acts with a pure thought, joy follows him, like a shadow that never leaves. The thought manifests as the word. The word manifests as the deed. The deed develops into habit. And the habit hardens into character. So watch the thought and your words with care, and let them spring from love, born out of concern for all beings. People will hear your words and be influenced by them for good or ill. They have the immense power to both heal and destroy. When words are both true and kind, they can change our world.

Yours,

Buddha Bhai

Tom and Martha's first daughter, also named Martha, was born September 27, 1772. Tom now found himself both a husband and a father, having to balance family life with all of his new political responsibilities.

December 5, 1772

Dear Thomas,

It was great to finally see you again. What a beautiful family you now have. A family is a place where minds come in contact with one another. If these minds love one another, the home will be as beautiful as a flower garden. But if these minds get out of harmony with one another, it is like a storm that plays havoc with the garden. In the end, there is only love. Beyond this, *there is nothing. It is the most powerful force in the universe. When all is said and done, what is there but love? It conquers everything.*

The most worthy personal aim one can have, Thomas, is to keep up the quest to perfect themselves spiritually. Just as a candle cannot burn without fire, so man cannot live without a spiritual life. It is better to conquer yourself than to win a thousand battles. Then the victory is yours. It cannot be taken from you, not by angels or demons, heaven or hell.

Yours,

Buddha Bhai

Tom never let his rapid rise to prominence go to his head. His constituents were struck by his simplicity and down-to-earth manner. He always dressed simply and neatly, avoiding any signs of extravagance or wealth. Although soft-spoken and mild-mannered, he came across as decisive to his colleagues in the House. Above all, he believed in sincerity, honesty, and respect in all his interactions— whatever a person's political views.

"He who permits himself to tell a lie once, finds it much easier to do it a second and third time, till at length it becomes habitual; he tells lies without attending to it, and truths without the world's believing him. . . . This falsehood of the tongue leads to that of the heart, and in time depraves all its good dispositions. . . . An honest heart being the first blessing, a knowing head is the second. . . . In matters of style, swim with the current; in matters of principle, stand like a rock."

Observing the day-to-day business in the House, Tom found the atmosphere to be unnecessarily formal and stuffy. He put forward a number of suggestions, with the aim of transforming it into a friendlier and less intimidating place. He advocated for no official titles, preferring the title "Mister" as opposed to "Your Excellency" for anyone in charge of a committee. He liked the simple habit of shaking hands rather than bowing to leaders.

Tom also came to the conclusion that it was best to have vigorous checks and balances, with stringent term limits for all House members—unlike the aristocracy that exercised excessive power. He believed that a ruling monarchy divided people into two classes, "the wolves and the sheep," and wanted the distance between the rulers and the ruled to be as small as possible. He proposed allowing the general public into the elected institutions, to see firsthand how their representatives worked.

Many of Tom's colleagues appreciated these new and radical ideas, but others were not so enthusiastic. He learned all too quickly that in politics, people could instantaneously turn against him when they perceived a threat. He was inexperienced and still very sensitive at heart, deeply hurt when those whom he counted as friends turned on him.

"The glow of one warm thought is to me worth more than money. . . . I find the pain of a little censure, even when it is unfounded, is more acute than the pleasure of much praise."

February 3, 1773

Dear Thomas,

I understand your disappointment at some of the nastiness from your peers. An insincere and evil friend is more to be feared than a wild beast; a wild beast may wound your body, but an evil friend will wound your mind.

Yours,

Buddha Bhai

Some who witnessed Tom's increasing influence tried to take advantage of him, and he was regularly asked for favors and showered with gifts, which he consistently but politely declined to accept. Tom worked tirelessly to understand the nature of societies and what the best system of governing would entail. He arrived at the conclusion that any government would only work if it supported the best traits in its people.

"There is a natural aristocracy among men. The grounds of this are virtue and talents. . . . He who knows nothing is closer to the truth than he whose mind is filled with falsehoods and errors. . . . It is error alone which needs the support of government. Truth can stand by itself. . . . A wise and frugal government, which shall restrain men from injuring one another, which shall leave them otherwise free to regulate their own pursuits of industry and improvement, and shall not take from the mouth of labor the bread it has earned. This is the sum of good government."

The majority of the Burgess members came from wealthy and privileged backgrounds. Tom harbored no great desire to accumulate money and liked to spend whatever he had generously, usually on everyone around him. He was uncomfortable with there being a wide wealth divide. The House needed to make important decisions on fiscal policy in Virginia and the allocation of funds. Tom felt a general suspicion toward bankers and opposed borrowing large sums, which could create long-term debt and dangerous speculation.

"Never spend your money before you have it. . . . While I wish to have every thing good in its kind, and handsome in stile, I am a great enemy to waste and useless extravagance, and see them with real pain. . . . We must not let our rulers load us with perpetual debt."

In May 1773, Tom's best friend since boyhood, Dabney Carr, succumbed to a blood infection. He was buried on the grounds of Monticello, as Tom had promised him. Two weeks later, tragedy struck again when Martha's father died, leaving the family in heavy debt and also making Tom the second largest slave owner in Albemarle County. The institution of slavery remained one of the greatest injustices of the day, and was a controversial topic.

"Under the law of nature, all men are born free, every one comes into the world with a right to his own person, which includes the liberty of moving and using it at his own will. . . . I tremble for my country when I reflect that God is just, that his justice cannot sleep forever. . . . The spirit of the master is abating, that of the slave rising from the dust . . . I hope preparing, under the auspices of heaven, for a total emancipation."

June 16, 1773

Dear Thomas,

You ask what I think of slavery. We have a saying that three things cannot be long hidden; the sun, the moon, and the truth.

Yours,

Buddha Bhai

Tom treated his slaves as well as he could, even including them as the "number of souls" in his family in the census— something that raised many eyebrows. He made multiple attempts to bring an end to the practice, putting forth a number acts. One such act failed by just a single vote. Many were unsympathetic to the cause, particularly those in the South. With the other political storm of the day raging, the time had not yet arrived for this fight.

"A good cause is often injured more by ill-timed efforts of its friends than by the arguments of its enemies. . . . The voice of a

single individual . . . would have prevented this abominable crime from spreading. . . . Thus we see the fate of millions unborn hanging on the tongue of one man . . . and heaven was silent in that awful moment! But it is to be hoped it will not always be silent and that the friends to the rights of human nature will, in the end, prevail. . . . No person hereafter coming into this country shall be held within the same in slavery under any pretext whatever. . . . This abomination must have an end. And there is a superior bench reserved in heaven for those who hasten it."

August 1, 1773

Dear Thomas,

Do not lose heart. Virtue is often persecuted more by the wicked than it is loved by the good.

Yours,

Buddha Bhai

The subject of religion was another hotly debated topic. What role should it play in daily politics? Tom visited church and drew inspiration from the Bible, but was reluctant to reveal his own beliefs in public. He was an ardent proponent of religious freedom; after all, the colonies had been founded on its very principles. It bothered him when he saw some of his colleagues trying to mix politics with religion.

*"The subject of religion, a subject on which I have ever been most
scrupulously reserved. I have considered it as a matter between
every man and his maker in which no other, and far less the public,
had a right to intermeddle. . . . Say nothing of my religion. It is
known to God and myself alone. Its evidence before the world is to
be sought in my life: if it has been honest and dutiful to society the
religion which has regulated it cannot be a bad one."*

The House received communication that Parliament had passed the Tea Act. This kept in place a three-penny-per-pound import tax on tea and controversially gave the struggling near-bankrupt British East India Company a virtual monopoly on tea sales. The company would now be able to sell to only their favored merchants—to the exclusion of other American traders. A mass protest broke out in Philadelphia, with similar reactions in other cities. A significant number of British tea agents were forced to resign, but those in Massachusetts continued at their jobs. When three ships full of tea arrived in Boston harbor, local meetings convened to discuss what to do with their cargo. It was decided to send the tea on one ship, the *Dartmouth*, back to England without paying any import duties. Governor Hutchinson objected strongly, insisting the duties be paid and the tea unloaded. (Incidentally, members of his own family were involved in selling the tea.)

On December 16, 1773, Sam Adams addressed a crowd of eight thousand Bostonians at the Old South Meeting House to inform them of the governor's decision. That very same night a group of men dressed up as Mohawk Indians boarded the ships and peacefully dumped hundreds of tea chests into the harbor.

December 17, 1773

Dear Thomas,

I couldn't help but get caught up in the events last night in Boston. I was one of the Mohawks! A peaceful, coordinated demonstration by the local people. I have a feeling that this event may be talked about for many years to come.

Yours,

Buddha Bhai

VI

Both Crown and Parliament were enraged when they received news of the Tea Party. A loud clamor in Britain to exact a swift revenge on the colonies, singling out rebellious Massachusetts for punishment, led to a series of Coercive Acts.

- The Boston Port Act shut down all commercial shipping in Boston until Massachusetts compensated the East India Company and paid the taxes owed on the destroyed tea.

- The Massachusetts Government Act gave more power to the Royal governor, transferring it out of the hands of the colonists and restricting the number of town meetings they could hold.

- The Administration of Justice Act protected Crown officials from being tried by local courts.

The situation got even worse when the Quebec Act extended the Canadian border southwards into colonial territory and the Quartering Act was extended. General Thomas Gage, supreme commander of the British army in North America, was made governor of Massachusetts, replacing Governor Hutchinson.

The colonists were stunned, and promptly started calling these new measures the *Intolerable Acts*.

February 21, 1774

Dear Thomas,

I fear that I may not be able to write to you for much longer. The purpose for which we came to the Americas is nearing its end. I regret to inform you that my life is now in danger. They know of my existence and our correspondence, and consider me a great threat. The new Governor Gage himself has dispatched a battalion of elite troops to find me. I would like to meet you very soon. Will you be at home for the next week?

Yours,

Buddha Bhai

Bhai had indeed found himself in some trouble. His traveling had been discovered, and one of his letters to Tom had been intercepted. The powers that be were not happy with this strange foreigner wandering the colonies.

March 16, 1774

Dear Thomas,

Thank you for meeting us and for your offer of help. It fills me with delight to know that you are having such marvelous ideas. I am also heartened by your belief that our exchanges over the years have helped you greatly. There is no need to thank me at all, it has been an honor, for you are the one who has done all the hard work. No one saves us but ourselves, no one can and no one may. We alone must walk the path.

The Sixth Ancient Principle is to live a life of purpose. Indeed, a life without one is somewhat meaningless. We need a reason to get up every morning, something we really believe in. It is a travesty to just go through the motions.

Yours,

Buddha Bhai

May 9, 1774

Dear Thomas,

I only just received your last letter. I am sorry, but your question about purpose is one that I cannot answer for you. Only you are in possession of the answer. You are still young and have already come so far, forming strong opinions on a number of issues. Your mission should be something that you truly feel passionate about. We believe that the biggest purpose one can have *is to follow a noble and righteous cause, for people and country, dedicated to the service of others. A cause much bigger than yourself. Make not the acquisition of vast amounts of money, possessions, or land your ultimate goal. Greed begets more greed. Such is a miserable existence. You were brought up in a life of luxury, and had you wanted to, could have lived a life surrounded by indulgence and pleasures. But you wanted more than this and rejected the security of your comfort zone, did you not?*

When you shall find what you feel passionate about and make it your life's work, then you will be elevated to a whole new rewarding level of existence and self-fulfillment. So, your work is to discover your work and then with all your heart to give yourself to it. Travel the path by becoming the path itself. And when you resolve to do this well, striving for excellence, then success will chase you.

Yours,

Buddha Bhai

Upon hearing of the Intolerable Acts, Tom was devastated that the colonies continued to be subject to such oppression. Since his election to the House, his eloquence—especially with his pen—had impressed everyone, whether or not they agreed with his views. Tom now set about writing his true feelings on the political question of the day. He drafted a resolution to show solidarity with Massachusetts, proclaiming a day of "fasting and prayer." Then, in July 1774, he published *A Summary View of the Rights of British America*. This document stated emphatically that the British Parliament had *no* authority over the colonies, and that the colonists had the simple right of self-government.

"The God who gave us life, gave us liberty at the same time."

The document became extremely popular, being published far and wide, and even making its way to England. To his surprise, Tom became an overnight sensation. He had not expected it to be so successful and was taken aback and somewhat embarrassed by all the publicity. He was risking his life with what could be considered high treason against the King. Some of his ideas were even too radical for the other members of the House, who chided him for being so blunt. But Tom was not deterred, for the more he reflected upon everything, the more convinced he became of his own true purpose.

"I have sworn upon the altar of God eternal hostility against every form of tyranny over the mind of man."

In Massachusetts, the Suffolk Resolves were drawn up, pledging outright resistance to the Intolerable Acts. By now, all colonists agreed that a new, larger, united organization was necessary to stand up against the British Empire. In September 1774, the First Continental Congress was convened. Fifty-six delegates from all over the colonies met in the central city of Philadelphia. Some notable members included Sam Adams, John Adams, George Washington, and John Dickinson, to name but a few. They unanimously agreed that the Intolerable Acts should not be obeyed, and force would be used if necessary. Local militia were to be formed around Boston. They would be called "minutemen" because they could be ready for battle at a minute's notice if called upon.

Later, back in Virginia, the House held its meeting in a church in Richmond, where Patrick Henry made a stirring speech against British rule, exclaiming, "Give me liberty or give me death!" Tom sat spellbound at the front and led in a standing ovation.

The British became even more furious over the colonists' refusal to bow. They committed to completely isolate Massachusetts, starving her into submission. King George passed the New England Restraining Act, which required exclusive trade with Britain and severely restricted fishing rights. Governor Gage declared martial law.

November 26, 1774

Dear Thomas,

I am still here in Boston, and am sad to say that the situation appears to be rapidly deteriorating. My people always stand for peace, harmony, and reconciliation. But no one may clap with one hand. Unfortunately, from what I am seeing, confrontation now seems inevitable.

I read your Summary View with terrific pride, as did everyone else. Ultimately, an idea, no matter how noble, means nothing without action. We do not believe in a fate that falls on men however they act; but we do believe in a fate that falls on them unless they act. There are only two mistakes one can make along this road: not going all the way, and not starting. And the journey, Thomas, has already started.

Yours,

Buddha Bhai

Despite the Restraining Act, Massachusetts was far from cut off. Her sister colonies rallied around, helping to transport food to her people over land. When General Gage learned this and discovered the local militia activities, he and the military opted to get more aggressive. A plan was formulated to seize and destroy the colonists' weapons supplies in Lexington and Concord (both towns outside Boston) and arrest Sam Adams and John Hancock.

On April 18, 1775, a large battalion containing hundreds of elite soldiers gathered on Boston Common to prepare for the surprise attack. A local spy network had seen the preparations, and signals were sent via lantern in the Old North Church to show how the soldiers were advancing: "one if by land, and two if by sea." Paul Revere, the silversmith who had now become expert at riding messages, set off on horseback for the fifteen-mile ride to warn the colonists that the British were coming. He reached Lexington at midnight—just in time to alert Sam Adams and John Hancock, saving them from certain arrest and probable execution.

Early the next morning, the Redcoats arrived, only to realize that their attack was no surprise. They confronted a number of Massachusetts Patriot militiamen on Lexington green who refused to surrender. Shots were fired and eight colonists were killed. The British continued their march to Concord, where properties were searched to uncover and destroy weapons. But there they found that even more Patriots were putting up a fight. Many of them were local farmers who now found themselves fighting against trained soldiers, their simple rifles pitted against the soldiers' flintlocks. As the day wore on, increasing numbers joined in the defense of their land against the Redcoats. British reinforcements arriving from Boston were shot at from buildings and behind walls. So effective was the resistance that the soldiers at Concord were eventually forced into a long retreat back to Boston. They were attacked the whole way, sustaining a large number of casualties. Little did they know that the advancing Patriots were about to lay siege to the city.

April 19, 1775

Dear Thomas,

I saw that wonderful talented man, Mr. Revere, race past me on his horse last night! There was a lot of commotion afterwards. I am sure by now you must have read about the events of today. All I can say is that the earth has been shaken. They are already calling the first Lexington battle a "shot heard 'round the world". So much activity and now a tense military standoff. Everyone here senses and feels it. America will never be the same again.

Yours,

Buddha Bhai

The Second Continental Congress convened in May 1775. Tom's performance in the House of Burgesses and his fame following *A Summary View* led to his being nominated as a delegate from Virginia. He left for Philadelphia on horseback, the journey taking well over a week on the dirt track. On the arrival of this youthful six-foot-two-inch slender man, people were struck by how sensible and distinguished he looked for his age, with a distinct, quiet charm about him. Tom was one of the youngest members, being only thirty-two years old. He had barely traveled out of his home colony of Virginia yet he was taking his seat among some of the biggest names of the colonies. John Adams, on working with him, commented that he was "tough as a lignum vitae knot. . . . Though a silent member of congress, he was so prompt, frank, explicit, and decisive upon committees and in conversation . . . that he soon seized upon my heart."

Tom was certainly shy and quiet at first, not a natural public speaker. But he was extremely hard working and dedicated to the cause. Another delegate, who had not been present during the First Continental Congress, was also deeply impressed with him—a certain distinguished gentleman now back in America, by the name of Benjamin Franklin.

June 1, 1775

Dear Thomas,

You worry that you are no public speaker. Despair not. We have a saying that a dog is not considered a good dog because he is a good barker. Similarly, a man is not considered a good man because he is a good talker.

Yours,

Buddha Bhai

John Hancock was elected president of the Congress. The delegates agreed that following the events in Massachusetts, it was necessary to create a new Continental Army that would represent all the colonies, as opposed to the local disorganized militia that had been fighting in Lexington and Concord. John Adams took the floor and put forward George Washington to be made commander-in-chief of the army. He was a man well respected by everyone in Congress and admired for his heroics in the frontier wars. Washington humbly accepted the position with the support of the delegates. Other military officers were then appointed, including some retired British officers who opposed King George III.

Heavy weapons were still in scarce supply for the Patriots after the Battles of Lexington and Concord, so a plan was hatched to capture Fort Ticonderoga in upstate New York, which contained a large weapons cache. A small force of Green Mountain Boys—the Patriot militia in New Hampshire—led by a brave man named Ethan Allen, marched on the fort and easily overwhelmed its soldiers. It had been poorly defended, and the British could only look on with surprise as the fort was taken.

Meanwhile, the tense standoff continued in Boston, as the British were trapped in the city. On June 17, over twelve hundred Patriot militiamen dug out a fortification on the high ground of Breed's Hill. They had been watching their opponents' preparations and were expecting to face a large assault by land and sea. The navy opened fire, and soon Charlestown was completely ablaze. After waiting for a few hours, over two thousand British soldiers charged up the hill. The colonists were given the order, "Do not fire until you see the whites of their eyes!" When the Redcoats were within a few feet, the Patriots opened fire—forcing them into a retreat back down the hill.

A second attempt by the British shortly afterwards produced the same result, as the Patriots took advantage of their high ground position. But the British were not going to give up, especially with their larger numbers. The third time they attacked, they succeeded in capturing the hill, after the Americans ran out of ammunition. But their victory came at a cost—with 226 dead and several hundred wounded. The Americans lost 115 men, including General Joseph Warren, the physician who helped inoculate thousands of Bostonians against smallpox.

July 10, 1775

Dear Thomas,

I have been hearing about your progress intently, and can see that you are now following your true passions and beliefs. Sorry that you are feeling down over the defeat at Breed's Hill. I saw the whole fight unfold and the terrific spirit of your people. The odds may be against you with the might of the army you face, but no task is too great. It is only during adversity that we are truly tested, and every setback in life is also an opportunity. I told you that we are scholars of all world religions. Is there not a saying in the Bible: "Truly I tell you, if you have faith the size of a mustard seed, and you will say to the mountain, Move! And it will move . . . nothing is impossible." Don't ever give up no matter how improbable the odds may seem. Whatever you are doing in life, belief in success or failure is often a self-fulfilling prophecy. Have no fear, my friend.

Yours,
Buddha Bhai

Although the so-called Battle of Bunker Hill was lost, American morale was boosted in the knowledge that the highly experienced British soldiers had to work so hard for their victory. They were some of the world's most exclusive troops fighting against mostly novice farmers and locals.

Two weeks after the battle, General Washington arrived to take command of seventeen thousand men in Cambridge who would form the core of the new Continental Army. The men had been sent from across the colonies, though they were still ill-equipped and poorly trained.

On July 5 the Continental Congress put forward the Olive Branch Petition, drafted by John Dickinson. This petition attempted reconciliation with Britain by appealing directly to the Crown. The petition was carried to London by Richard Penn, the grandson of William Penn. Far from being interested in a compromise, however, King George refused to even look at the petition and instead declared the Americans to be in an open state of rebellion. He labeled them traitors and issued a royal proclamation to forcefully quell the unrest, punishing any rebels by hanging. Additional suppressive measures were passed to completely shut down the colonies to all trade. General William Howe replaced Thomas Gage as commander-in-chief of the British forces.

Word of the king's snub reached America by the end of the year. There seemed to be no turning back now from military conflict.

The Royal Navy began bombarding the East Coast, decimating the town of Falmouth, Massachusetts. By December, there were 27,500 enlisted Continental Army soldiers under the command of General Washington. But the odds were still against them because of Britain's vastly superior reserves and finances. The magnitude of the task was made obvious by the difference between the navies. The British had the mightiest fleet in the world, with hundreds of warships. The colonists, by contrast, didn't even have an established navy. The British military was also swelled by thousands of Hessians, German mercenaries fighting for the Crown.

The Continental Army bravely tried to take the fight to the British, attempting an invasion of Canada, but this offensive was unsuccessful, and they were forced into a quick retreat. Henry Knox, a Boston bookstore owner, now turned colonel, came up with the idea of transporting the heavy artillery captured from Fort Ticonderoga to Cambridge, three hundred miles away, to shore up the Patriot defenses. The future of this courageous struggle was far from certain.

VII

It had now been over fifteen years since Tom first met Bhai.

January 2, 1776

Dear Thomas,

Happy New Year! I am certain that this will be a colossal year. We have evaded the most brutal of forces arrayed against us, managing to escape. Sadly, I have lost several more of my people. My time in this great land of yours is at an end, and I shall be sailing back East soon. I have our final and Seventh Ancient Principle to share with you.

This is all about the pursuit of happiness, which is the ultimate purpose of life, is it not? It is certainly right to say that almost everything we do is in the name of its attainment. So how do we arrive at this state of mind we call happiness?

Actually, there is no one single secret to achieving it. But here is what we believe. That if you shall practice all the Ancient

Principles consistently, you will be best placed to get there. When you treat your body well, thirst for knowledge, practice discipline, stay calm, are of good character, and pursue your passions—then happiness will come to you. You shall no longer need to search for it.

Yours,

Buddha Bhai

January 15, 1776

Dear Thomas,

As I get ready to leave, I wish to remind you to continue to strive for excellence, and to share all of my lessons with others too. Thousands of candles can be lit from a single candle, and the life of the candle will not be shortened. Happiness never decreases by being shared. Teach this triple truth to all: A generous heart, kind speech, and a life of service and compassion are the things which renew humanity. If you light a lamp for somebody, it will also brighten your path.

Yours,

Buddha Bhai

In January 1776, New Hampshire adopted the first American state constitution. Shortly thereafter, North Carolina allowed its delegates to work toward full independence. In Philadelphia, an Englishman named Thomas Paine, who himself had immigrated to

America only a year before, published a pamphlet that heavily criticized the king and monarchy, calling for a complete break from Britain. The publication, *Common Sense*, became an instant best–seller, with the famous conclusion, "We have it in our power to begin the world over again. A situation, similar to the present, hath not happened since the days of Noah until now. The birthday of a new world is at hand." Hundreds of thousands of copies were sold across the colonies. Paine used common, easy-to-understand language to make his case appealing to his readers. Tom read the document back home in Monticello, and was delighted that its theories were so well received.

More good news was around the corner. Henry Knox was successful in his plan to transport the heavy artillery, including fifty canons, from Fort Ticonderoga back to Boston using sleds pulled by over 150 oxen. As a result, the Americans were able to fortify the strategically important location of Dorchester Heights. The British realized they had been outwitted and surrounded, and would no longer be able to hold onto the city. Finally, General Howe withdrew his army and naval fleet, fleeing to Nova Scotia.

February 29, 1776

Dear Thomas,

Happiness does not lie in some distant point in the future, but is accessible at any moment you choose. Focus on the present moment always, and all the opportunities you have right here and now. Not tomorrow, but today. Every moment not spent on happiness is a moment wasted. The best things in our lives that produce happiness are simultaneously free and priceless. They are also accessible at any moment, from spending time with family, seeing a loved one smile, watching the sunset, or enjoying a simple stroll experiencing the awesome beauty of nature. There is, after all, so much happiness to be gained this very second.

The pursuit of happiness is what it's all about, Mr. Thomas Jefferson. I wish you well in all your future endeavors.

Yours,

Buddha Bhai

Tom had been through his share of ups and downs over the past few years, and his own experiences had given him insight into what it truly meant to be happy. He had been blessed with many wonderful things in life and was grateful. But there was urgent work to be done.

At the beginning of June, a resolution for complete independence was proposed by the Virginia delegate, Richard Henry Lee; "That these United Colonies are, and of right ought to be, free and Independent States, that they are absolved from all allegiance to the British Crown, and that all political connection between them and the State of Great Britain is, and ought to be, totally dissolved." Congress recognized that the time had now arrived to formally take this monumental step. When only nobility ruled over other nations, here stood a group of mostly regular men, taking a stand against oppression, demanding their rights to liberty and self-rule. For the first time in history, a nation based on an idea was to be born.

On June 11, a small committee was formed to prepare a declaration. The members consisted of Benjamin Franklin, John Adams, Roger Sherman, Robert Livingston—and Tom. Benjamin Franklin was the most senior member of the group, and Tom one of the youngest. Aware of Tom's supreme talents, John Adams persuaded him to take on the task of writing the declaration. "Reason first, you are a Virginian, and a Virginian ought to appear at the head of this business. Reason second, I am obnoxious, suspected, and unpopular. You are very much otherwise. Reason third, you can write ten times better than I can."

Tom graciously accepted and got right to work. Being a visionary, his aim was to express in his own words not only a bold proclamation for the colonies, but also the greatest aspirations for the *whole* of mankind. He wrote in his small room, meticulously going over each word and sentence—editing and re-editing. Within just a few days, his text was complete. The document was passed around and looked over by the other members of the committee. They were astonished at the power of Tom's words, which brought tears to many eyes. Just over two weeks later, the declaration was presented to the rest of Congress.

On July 2, twelve of the thirteen colonial delegations voted in support of Richard Henry Lee's resolution for independence, with only New York abstaining. Their focus then moved on to Tom's declaration. The members debated the exact wording for two days. A big omission, insisted on by some of the other members of Congress, was a passage on the slave trade.

"He has waged cruel war against human nature itself, violating its most sacred rights of life & liberty in the persons of a distant people who never offended him, captivating & carrying them into slavery in another hemisphere, or to incur miserable death in their transportation thither."

It was observed that during the debate, Tom said little himself, preferring democratic agreement among the delegates. But he was certainly disappointed that many of his colleagues didn't see fit to agree with him on slavery.

On July 4, 1776, Congress formally ratified Tom's declaration: *A Declaration by the Representatives of the United States of America, in General Congress Assembled.* A moment of reflection, and then the delegates recorded their signatures. This was an act of treason if the revolution failed; the delegates knew that they were risking everything.

As a true Enlightenment thinker, Tom saw the good in human spirit, and hoped that the government could embody that vision. He had chosen his words very carefully. "Life, liberty, and property" was a phrase that had been used before, and it didn't seem to encompass all that he wanted for his people's well-being. Although he would never see or hear from his secret mentor again, Tom knew that he would have been proud if he had seen the wording.

"When in the Course of human events it becomes necessary for one people to dissolve the political bands which have connected them with another and to assume among the powers of the earth, the separate and equal station to which the Laws of Nature and of Nature's God entitle them, a decent respect to the opinions of mankind requires that they should declare the causes which impel them to the separation. We hold these truths to be self-evident, that all men are created equal, that they are endowed by their Creator with certain unalienable Rights, that among these are Life, Liberty and the pursuit of Happiness."

Unbeknownst to Tom though, Buddha Bhai was already standing in that Philadelphia crowd smiling and cheering when the Declaration of Independence of the United States of America was read.

The story the Himalayan sage told had captivated me, as well as reminding me of the heroics of the American Revolution. Certainly the sages were convinced, and I held the letters in my hands as proof. Upon my return to Boston, my own research revealed some interesting facts.

Tom did undoubtedly go off course after his father passed away, and he began to excel again only after he had been in college for some time. His mother, Jane Randolph Jefferson, is not well documented. In fact, very little is known of her. That seemed odd to me, considering she bore one of the most famous Americans of all time. Was she deliberately banished from the history books? The sages told me that she read many of Buddha Bhai's letters, and became quite an ardent follower of his. If this had become known, many people would have likely viewed her with suspicion and even fear—possibly believing such new ideas to border on the occult. It had, after all, been only a few decades since the infamous Salem Witch trials.

When we take an in-depth look at all of his lifestyle practices, we see that Tom practiced very Eastern ways of living, quite different from his fellow countrymen. In many ways he was a well-being guru, centuries ahead of his time. His recommendations are the same as those most physicians would be proud to promote today.

By basing his diet primarily on vegetables, Tom consumed abundant amounts of vitamins, minerals, fiber, and antioxidants. His diet was unusually low in meat, at a time when red meat, especially, was popular. Research now proves the wide-ranging health benefits of eating a diet rich in fruits and vegetables, primarily a plant-based rather than meat-based diet.

Tom later developed an avid love for olives, calling the plant "the richest gift of heaven . . . the most interesting plant in existence." He regularly used olive oil and went on to manufacture sesame seed oil. Both of these vegetable oils are high in polyunsaturated fats, which contain the "good" high-density cholesterol that helps to lower the "bad" low-density cholesterol. He was also a red wine connoisseur, frequently drinking it with his meals, calling that "wine . . . indispensible for my health." Interestingly, both red wine and olive oil form part of the Mediterranean diet, which is currently recommended as a healthy way of eating.

Just as importantly, Tom practiced great temperance even though he had access to many exotic foods and delicacies. He never believed in overeating—a common problem at the time for the more privileged (as evident by portraits of John Adams and Benjamin

Franklin). His healthy habits even extended to the way he ate his meals. He insisted on dining with his family around the dinner table, a traditional custom that has sadly become a rarity and has been shown by sociological research to undermine family cohesion.

Tom always endeavored to spread his dietary beliefs to those around him. When he was asked to plan a menu for students at the University of Virginia, he included large amounts of wheat (high in fiber) and milk (high in calcium), and a wide variety of vegetables. He advised plenty of water and "no stimulating drinks, and the habit of using them being dangerous." Most authorities now agree that we do not drink anywhere near enough pure water, the result being that we instead consume more sugary high-calorie drinks. The stimulant drink industry has become a multi-billion-dollar enterprise, including the quick-energy drinks that have become popular among young people. Many of these have been shown to be alarmingly high in both caffeine and sugar.

Regular outdoor walking was a habit that Tom believed was essential for his well-being. Health organizations class brisk walking as moderate physical activity, of which at least two and a half hours a week is recommended. The fact that Tom was aspiring to do two hours a day indicates just how far he strived to stay active. Back then, he could already see the trend towards a more sedentary lifestyle and was concerned that mechanized processes would make people lazier. Today, of course, we are much worse—with our cars, televisions, and computers, all leading to less physical activity. Regular exertion has a number of proven health benefits for all age groups. People who exercise are also naturally in better shape with lower rates of obesity. In addition, there are numerous positive mental and emotional effects. During exercise, endorphins are released within the brain in large quantities, producing a general feeling of euphoria and well-being, an elevation in mood, and reduced symptoms of depression and stress. Scientists have even confirmed lower rates of neurodegenerative illness and improved intellectual capacity.

Tom's favorite hobby of gardening involved gentle stretching exercises and spending time in the fresh air. This popular outdoor activity has several advantages, including a proven blood pressure–lowering effect. The weather in the mid-Atlantic region was much the same as it is now, with warm, sunny weather for several months during the summer—certainly not as harsh as the weather some of his colleagues endured in New England.

The devastating health effects of smoking would not become apparent to the scientific community until the late twentieth century, yet Tom had the amazing foresight to suspect that it was an unhealthy habit. His questioning attitude toward doctors was refreshing for the time; he sincerely desired to see only evidence-based medicine practiced.

The frequent use of meditative techniques, whether formal meditation or mindfulness techniques while doing other activities such as walking, is another valuable practice. Studies show these techniques can help decrease stress, elevate mood, and even relieve physical pain. If Tom practiced this type of mindfulness activity for a couple of hours a day while he walked, it likely did him an immense amount of good. Tom later made a second home in a more peaceful setting, Poplar Forest, Virginia—specifically with the aim of using it as a relaxation retreat.

Researchers have investigated the ideal amount of necessary sleep, and have concluded that the optimal amount is between six and eight hours. Too little sleep and too much sleep have both been associated with adverse health outcomes. At a time when people are sleeping less and finding restful sleep more difficult to attain, we can learn a lot from Tom. He kept himself extremely busy and packed a lot of activities into his typical day, which meant that he was usually tired by bedtime. He stuck to a regular routine and did not sleep at erratic times. He would typically read before he slept, which experts advocate is an excellent way to calm the mind before switching off the lights.

Tom was a dedicated "morning lark," a characteristic shared by many successful people. The merits and drawbacks of being either a morning lark or a "night owl" have been debated, with conflicting theories. With certainty, however, we can say that by rising early, Tom would have been able to accomplish more during the day—by giving himself those extra few hours each morning. He later boasted that in fifty years, "the sun had never caught him in bed."

Another good habit that Tom formed was bathing regularly. This was unusual for the time but was obviously great for personal hygiene. Benjamin Franklin, for instance, used to simply take "air baths" instead of using water!

On a personal level, Tom displayed a number of virtuous characteristics. He was highly motivated by the desire to do good for his people and country, and rarely by more extrinsic factors such as money or prestige. He was an extremely social person and delighted in being around people and entertaining guests. His daughter Martha recalled having as many as fifty guests at a time in the twelve-bedroom Monticello. Moreover, Tom was the ultimate optimist, embodying the ideals of the Revolution. Fascinating studies have revealed that all of these character traits—intrinsic motivation, sociability, and optimism—result in improved well-being measures, including longevity, success, and happiness.

It comes as no surprise, then, that with all of his terrific practices and attributes, Tom was blessed with good health throughout his life. His biggest problems arose from a wrist he broke in Paris and odd headaches and minor chest colds he suffered from every few years. When he was older, he confirmed that he had kept well and had "not yet lost a tooth by age." Tom lived to the age of eighty-three, at a time when the average life expectancy was only thirty-five years. He lived much longer than anyone else in his family. His enlightened principles of living were able to nurture his great mind, and in so doing he helped establish the founding of

America.

With my newfound knowledge of Thomas Jefferson, I resolved to tell the world what he could teach us about health and well-being.

To this day, Tom remains an enigma. His name is ingrained in the psyche of every American from elementary school. Institutions across the land have been named in his honor. His stare pierces us every time we look at a nickel or the rare two-dollar bill. His face is etched on Mount Rushmore. One of the largest memorials in Washington, DC, modeled on the Pantheon, is dedicated to him. Yet it was not simply his ascent to the highest office in the land that made Tom such an iconic figure.

Few in world history could claim a list of talents and achievements as diverse as his. He was a scientist, inventor, lawyer, writer, farmer, architect, violinist, surveyor, archaeologist, philosopher, botanist, and linguist. He could read and write in English, French, Spanish, Italian, Greek, and Latin. Tom was even known to practice medicine. The historical term to describe a single individual with such an incredible array of expertise is *polymath*— putting him in the same league as Leonardo da Vinci. The prominent nineteenth-century biographer, James Parton, wrote that by his early thirties Tom "could calculate an eclipse, survey an estate, tie an artery, plan an edifice, try a case, break a horse, dance a minuet, and play the violin."

The Declaration of Independence did not, of course, mark the end of the Revolution. The war raged on even as Tom was writing those famous words. The British were not going to let go of their prized colonies so easily. Congress attempted to block all British shipping traffic, but a huge naval fleet arrived in New York, consisting of thirty battleships and thousands of soldiers. The Americans received an enormous diplomatic boost when France and Spain pledged their support. The fighting then continued on the mainland, with a series of American setbacks and advances for the next several years.

In 1779, Tom was elected governor of Virginia. Two years later the British briefly occupied Monticello; he narrowly escaped minutes before they arrived. The Revolutionary War finally ended in 1783 after the Treaty of Paris, and the United States took her place as a fully independent republic. A year later, Tom wrote his book *Notes on the State of Virginia*.

In total, he helped draft over one hundred bills—including the bills for the More General Diffusion of Knowledge, and the Statute of Virginia for Religious Freedom—which reformed the public education system and guaranteed respect for all faiths with separation of the state from religion.

Tom was appointed minister to France in 1784. Initially, he was not fond of France and its monarchy, but he soon warmed to the country as it edged closer to revolution. He stayed until 1789, during which time the US Constitution was drawn up and George Washington was sworn in as president in the capital, New York City.

Tom was appointed Secretary of State in 1790, overseeing what was then a tiny department. When Washington retired in 1796, Tom ran for president but was narrowly defeated by John Adams. Under the Constitution at the time, the person with the second largest number of electoral votes became vice president.

In 1798, France captured American ships trading with England, and the Alien and Sedition Acts were passed, giving the government power to suppress protesters and arrest and deport citizens, particularly those suspected of siding with France. Tom was horrified with such draconian measures, furthering the rift that was developing between himself and President Adams. Later he would personally pardon all those who were affected by the Act. His friendship with John Adams would only be rekindled many years later when the two started regularly corresponding again through a series of letters.

In the 1800 presidential election, Tom ran as a Democrat-Republican, advocating for less central control and more power with the states and countryside. His opponents, the Federalists, advocated for greater federal power, cities, and industrialization.

"I am not a friend to a very energetic government. It is always oppressive."

The election was close—Tom and Aaron Burr were tied, with John Adams third. The decision of who to elect President fell to the House of Representatives. Ironically, the war veteran and former treasury secretary Alexander Hamilton, a long-time critic of Tom, helped the decision to go in his favor.

News of Tom's election was well received across the country. Unlike George Washington, who arrived at his inauguration in a spectacular horse-drawn coach, Tom arrived alone on horseback in the new capital (named after Washington). He was dressed plainly and stayed at a simple boardinghouse. It was not his style to absorb himself in pomp or ceremony. Tom took the oath of office in the new capitol building on March 4,th 1801, and gave his inaugural address.

"Let us, then, fellow citizens, unite with one heart and one mind. . . harmony and affection without which liberty and even life itself are but dreary things. . . . Every difference of opinion is not a difference of principle. . . freedom of religion; freedom of the press, and freedom of person under the protection of the habeas corpus, and trial by juries impartially selected. These principles form the bright constellation which has gone before us and guided our steps through an age of revolution and reformation. The wisdom of our sages and blood of our heroes have been devoted to their attainment. . . should

we wander from them in moments of error or of alarm, let us hasten to retrace our steps, and to regain the road which alone leads to peace, liberty, and safety. . . . Relying, then, on the patronage of your good will, I advance with obedience to the work. . . . And may that Infinite Power which rules the destinies of the universe lead our councils to what is best."

Tom wanted the United States to be a beacon of hope and liberty to the whole world. His presidency occurred at a crucial moment, as international conflict between Britain and France threatened to destabilize the young nation. His time in office was significant for a number of defining events. In 1801, the First Barbary War started against pirates in the Mediterranean who were attacking American ships. In 1803, Jefferson made the Louisiana Purchase from Napoleon. With the stroke of a pen, he purchased land from France, which more than doubled the size of the United States. The price paid was a bargain, just 15 million dollars, in one of the largest peaceful acquisitions of land in history. He announced this accomplishment to the American people on July 4.

Tom was re-elected president in 1804 by an overwhelming majority. In his second term, he supervised the Lewis and Clark expedition—the first large-scale archaeological exploration from the East Coast to the West Coast. It brought back a treasure trove of scientific and geographical information, and Tom was sent back boxes full of their discoveries.

In 1807 he passed the Embargo Act to maintain neutrality between Britain and France. Unfortunately, America still found it difficult to stay completely out of the war, and smuggling escalated. As his term neared its end, Tom's economic policies had helped cut the national debt substantially. He was asked to seek a third term, but he refused. He was revered by many but didn't want any special tributes like an official celebration of his birthday. In 1809 he rode out of Washington and returned home to Monticello.

Tom's passion for education continued throughout his life. When he sailed back to America from France in 1789, he brought with him dozens of crates full of books. At one stage he owned a significant number of all the books in circulation in the United States and later sold thousands of them to help found the Library of Congress. Tom believed strongly that only ability should determine one's educational opportunities—not wealth. He received thousands of letters and endeavored to reply to all of them, often requiring extensive research into the subject matter. Tom later founded the University of Virginia, and even designed the beautiful campus grounds.

"Enlighten the people generally, and tyranny and oppressions of body and mind will vanish like evil spirits at the dawn of day. . . .
When I contemplate the immense advances in science and discoveries. . . made within the period of my life, I look forward with confidence to equal advances by the present generation, and have no doubt they will consequently be as much wiser than we have been as we than our fathers were, and they than the burners of witches."

He continued to be interested in inventing. Some of his further inventions included a new type of plow that made harvesting easier, a wheel cipher that coded secret messages, a new type of spherical sundial, and a pedometer. He also helped perfect the design for a polygraph machine that made duplicate copies of all his letters.

Sadly, the institution of slavery continued to thrive in spite of Tom's many affirmations against the abhorrent practice. As president, he passed the Act Prohibiting Importation of Slaves, which effectively ended the Atlantic slave trade.

"I brought in a bill to prevent their further importation . . . leaving to future efforts its final eradication. . . . Persuasion, perseverance and patience are the best advocates on questions depending on the will of others. The revolution in public opinion which this cause requires, is not to be expected in a day, or perhaps in an age; but time, which outlives all things, will outlive this evil also."

His inheritance meant that he would still have a large number of slaves at Monticello, including one named Sally Hemmings, a controversy still debated to this day.

Tom had a lifelong interest in and admiration for Native American culture. He believed that Indians were noble and loyal. Tribal chiefs regularly visited him, and he displayed artifacts all over Monticello. The issue was complicated, however, since many of the

Indians had fought on the side of the British during the Revolutionary War. Tom had to balance Native rights against the ambitions of his new country to expand and populate. He knew that their way of life would never be the same in an expanding America and wished for assimilation. His stand on issues like this, and the fact that he continued to keep slaves himself, led some to say that Tom was a man of dichotomies and inconsistencies.

"None of us, no, not one, is perfect. And were we to love none who had imperfections, this world would be a desert for our love."

More than anything, Tom was devoted to his family. He disliked his absences from home, especially when his family did not write to him for a long time. Unfortunately, he suffered a number of personal tragedies throughout his life. Around the time of the writing of the Declaration, he lost both his second daughter and his mother. His beloved wife Martha died in 1782. Tom promised he would never remarry. In 1785, his youngest daughter died while he was in France. Only two of his six children survived to adulthood, and only his oldest daughter lived beyond the age of twenty-five, giving him eleven grandchildren. Yet despite these terrible losses, Tom showed amazing personal bravery, always returning to his duties for his country.

*"Whatever is to be our destiny, wisdom as well as duty, dictates
that we should acquiesce in the will of Him whose it is to give and
take away, and be contented in the enjoyment of those who are still
permitted to be with us."*

Monticello was never entirely completed—it remained a work in progress, much like the United States itself. The abolition of slavery would fall to another Secret Buddha student—Abraham Lincoln. He became a great fan of Tom's work, and often cited his quotes when talking about his own opposition.

Within a century and a half, the land of young, amateur fighters that took on a mighty empire would itself become the most powerful and prosperous nation in the world—one that would actually be called upon to rescue other continents from tyranny. The results of the Revolution and the Declaration of Independence served as an example for future generations that were fighting oppression. Years later, when Mahatma Gandhi was pitted against the same empire by rejecting the British salt tax, he proclaimed that the salt was "to remind us of the famous Boston Tea Party." He could well draw hope from Tom's words.

*"Trusted with the destinies of this solitary republic of the world,
the only monument of human rights, and the sole depository of the
sacred fire of freedom and self government, from hence it is to be
lighted up in other regions of the earth, if other regions of the earth
shall ever become susceptible of its benign influence. . . . And even
should the cloud of barbarism and despotism again obscure . . . this
country remains to preserve and restore light and liberty to them.*

*In short, the flames kindled on the 4 of July 1776, have spread over
too much of the globe to be extinguished by the feeble engines of
despotism; on the contrary, they will consume these engines and all
who work them."*

Tom died at home on July 4, 1826—on the fiftieth anniversary
of the Declaration. After his death, many of his possessions were
auctioned off and Monticello fell into disrepair. In 1834, the house
was bought by a Jewish naval officer who admired his contribution
to religious freedom.

Tom wanted only three achievements mentioned on the
memorial stone over his grave. The presidency was not one of them.

HERE WAS BURIED THOMAS JEFFERSON, AUTHOR OF THE
DECLARATION OF AMERICAN INDEPENDENCE, OF THE STATUTE
OF VIRGINIA FOR RELIGIOUS FREEDOM, AND FATHER OF THE
UNIVERSITY OF VIRGINIA. BORN APRIL 2 1743. DIED JULY 4 1826.

The spirit of self-belief from those dizzying days of
Revolution lives on. The time when a group of brave people from a
new and uncertain world came together from a diverse variety of
backgrounds to take on a mighty king and empire, standing up for
the simple cause of liberty. Today, millions continue to be inspired
by Thomas Jefferson, the genius who galvanized his people to
freedom. A truly enlightened soul indeed—and that, without ever
requiring any lessons from a Secret Buddha.

Other Pearls of Wisdom from the Great Mr. Jefferson

"No one knows, till he tries, how easily a habit of walking is acquired. A person who never walked three miles will in the course of a month become able to walk 15 or 20 without fatigue. I have known some great walkers and had particular accounts of many more; and I never knew or heard of one who was not healthy and long lived. . . . Should you be disposed to try it, as your health has been feeble, it will be necessary for you to begin with a little, and to increase it by degrees."

"I repeat my advice, to take a great deal of exercise, and on foot. Health is the first requisite after morality."

"A little walk of half an hour, in the morning, when you first rise, is advisable also. It shakes off sleep, and produces other good effects in the animal economy."

"The recipe . . . is simple diet, exercise and the open air . . . and we may venture to say that this recipe will give health and vigor to every other description."

"Exercise and application produce order in our affairs, health of body, cheerfulness of mind, and these make us precious to our friends."

"What I value more than all things, good humor."

"I look to the diffusion of light and education as the resource to be relied on for ameliorating the condition, promoting the virtue, and advancing the happiness of man."

"I know no safe depository of the ultimate powers of the society, but the people themselves; and if we think them not enlightened enough . . . the remedy is, not to take it from them, but to inform . . . by education. This is the true corrective of abuses of constitutional power."

"If a nation expects to be ignorant and free, in a state of civilization, it expects what never was and never will be."

"The man who reads nothing at all is better educated than the man who reads nothing but newspapers."

"It is your future happiness that interests me, and nothing can contribute more to it than the contracting a habit of industry and activity. Of all the cankers of human happiness none corrodes with so silent, yet so baneful a tooth, as indolence."

"Interesting occupations are essential to happiness."

"Never trouble another for what you can do for yourself."

"Do not bite at the bait of pleasure, till you know there is no hook beneath it."

"The majority, oppressing an individual, is guilty of a crime, abuses its strength, and by acting on the law of the strongest breaks up the foundations of society."

"Liberty . . . is the great parent of science and of virtue; and that a nation will be great in both always in proportion as it is free."

"Experience hath shewn that, even under the best forms . . . those entrusted with power have, in time, and by slow operations, perverted it into tyranny. . . . The most effectual means of preventing this would be, to illuminate . . . the minds of the people at large, and more especially to give them knowledge of those facts . . . that . . . of the experience of other ages and countries, they may be enabled to know ambition under all its shapes, and prompt to exert their natural powers to defeat its purposes."

"I would rather be exposed to the inconveniences attending too much liberty than to those attending too small a degree of it."

"Timid men prefer the calm of despotism to the tempestuous sea of liberty."

"What country can preserve its liberties if their rulers are not warned from time to time that their people preserve the spirit of resistance?"

"Pride costs us more than hunger, thirst and cold."

"Nor have I ever been able to conceive how any rational being could propose happiness to himself from the exercise of power over others."

"If we can but prevent the government from wasting the labours of the people, under the pretence of taking care of them, they must become happy."

"It is part of the American character to consider nothing as desperate—to surmount every difficulty by resolution and contrivance."

"Nothing is troublesome that we do willingly."

"Never put off till tomorrow what you can do today."

"Give up money, give up fame, give up science, give the earth itself and all it contains, rather than do an immoral act. And never suppose, that in any possible situation, or under any circumstances, it is best for you to do a dishonorable thing, however slightly so it may appear to you. Whenever you are to do a thing, though it can never be known but to yourself, ask yourself how you would act were all the world looking at you, and act accordingly."

All quotations in this book are taken from Thomas Jefferson's statements, publications, and letters to family, friends, and colleagues.

Many of Bhai's letters contain original sayings from Buddha.

Thank you, Mr. Jefferson, for the wonderful insights.

And of course, thank you Buddha.

CPSIA information can be obtained at www.ICGtesting.com
Printed in the USA
BVOW02s1731270116

434429BV00003B/210/P